"We only need one dog," Missus said.

"Just because we only need one doesn't mean we can't want two," Mister said. "And it doesn't mean we can't have two, either." He scratched with his fingers on the top of the black-and-white puppy's head.

Mine. Good.

"It's not as if we don't have room for two on the farm," Missus agreed, and she stroked the soft back of the white-and-sorrel puppy, all the way from her neck to the end of her tail.

Nice. Good. Yes.

"You have a farm?" the attendant asked. "Then you're perfect for these dogs."

So both puppies went home in the pickup truck with Mister and Missus, riding in a cardboard box behind the seat. It was strange to be in a box. They'd never been in a box before. They didn't know what to do. They didn't know what would happen, and the truck was so loud, it made them unhappy, uneasy. The little sorrel puppy climbed up on the big black-and-white one, and they both went to sleep.

CYNTHIA VOIGT

Angus
and
Sadie

Drawings by
Tom Leigh

HarperTrophy®
An Imprint of HarperCollins*Publishers*

Harper Trophy® is a registered trademark
of HarperCollins Publishers.

Angus and Sadie
Text copyright © 2005 by Cynthia Voigt
Illustrations copyright © 2005 by Tom Leigh
www.harpercollinschildrens.com

Library of Congress Cataloging-in-Publication Data
Voigt, Cynthia.
   Angus and Sadie / Cynthia Voigt ; drawings by Tom Leigh.—1st ed.
   p.   cm.
   Summary: Angus and Sadie, two siblings that are mostly
border collie heritage, are adopted by a young couple and start liv-
ing on a Maine farm, where they begin to learn sheep herding and
come to appreciate how they are different from each other.
   ISBN 978-0-06-074584-4
   1. Border collie—Juvenile fiction. [1. Border collie—Fiction.
2. Dogs—Fiction. 3. Farm life—Maine—Fiction. 4. Sheep herding—
Fiction. 5. Maine—Fiction.] I. Leigh, Tom, ill. II. Title.
PZ10.3.V928An 2005   2004018285
[Fic]—dc22
                               CIP
                               AC

Typography by Amy Ryan
14 15 OPM 10 9 8

First Harper Trophy edition, 2008

FOR MERRILEE HEIFETZ
(herself the mistress of a lively dog)
with thanks for her enthusiasm
and her continual wise counsel

For their help, however unwitting, thanks also:
to the big blacks, Emma and Calimero
to the boys, Poncho and Lefty
and to Vinnie, the original dancing dog

Contents

Angus and Sadie

1

How Mister and Missus
want a dog and decide to find one

Mister and Missus lived on a farm in Maine. The farm was called the Old Davis Place, because it had belonged to Mister's grandfather. When Old Mr. Davis died, he left the entire farm to his grandson, young Mr. Davis, and the farm kept its name.

The Old Davis Place was a big farm, one hundred and thirty-seven acres of woods and pastures and fields. It backed up against the mountains, so the farm had also some wide stony meadows, which in midsummer were covered with wild blueberries. Two streams ran down from the western mountains, crossing the farm on their way to a distant lake. The streams dug steep ravines out of the hills, and gulleys, too, before they joined together in the woods to make one slower, broader stream that meandered across the lower, flatter pastures and fields.

Mister and Missus raised sheep for wool and chickens for eggs. They kept two Guernsey cows, named Bethie and Annie after queens of England, for milk and butter and sometimes cheese. They planted alfalfa and hay, soybeans and feed corn in their fields. They grew vegetables in a big garden behind the house, and Missus also kept a few flower beds at the front. What they didn't need for themselves, they sold at a summer farm stand at the end of the driveway: vegetables and eggs and sometimes fresh butter. The alfalfa, hay, and corn that they didn't store for winter feed, they sold at the farmer's cooperative in town, as well as wool when they had it. All of the soybeans were sold at the cooperative; the soybeans were their cash crop.

Of course, there were cats on the farm. A farm needs cats. There were two barn cats, and they were hunters. They caught mice and rats, the occasional squirrel, and even the odd unlucky bird. A sleepy marmalade cat named Patches lived in the house, to catch the house mice.

Mister and Missus had sheep, cows, chickens, and cats, but they didn't have a dog. Sometimes they wondered if they might want one. So, one winter day, they went to the library and took out several books to learn about different breeds. They both read the books, and then on the long winter evenings while Missus cut squares of patterned cloth for a quilt and Mister sharpened the rototiller blades, they talked about the kind of dog they would want, if they wanted a dog.

Mister said, "I could train a dog to help herd the sheep and to find the milk cows when they wander off. A dog would keep the chickens safe from foxes and coyotes. The books say that border collies are easy to train, and they like to work hard."

Missus said, "A dog would keep deer out of my vegetable garden and raccoons out of the garbage. A dog would be company for me when you are away all day. The books say that border collies like being with people."

So it was decided. "We definitely need a dog and probably a border collie," Mister said.

"But a purebred dog is awfully expensive and, besides, I like mongrels. I like what happens when different breeds have mixed together to make something new."

"It looks like a border collie mongrel would be the perfect dog."

"Let's go to the animal shelter," Missus suggested.

"Not until spring, though. Not until we've moved the sheep out of their pen and up to the spring pasture."

"All right. In spring, we'll get our dog," said Missus.

At the animal shelter, the puppies lived in one big pen by the door, fourteen puppies from eight different litters, all together, all day long, all night long.

It was wonderful for those puppies to be in a big pen with so many friends to chew on and chase after and fight with over the heavy pieces of rope tied in thick knots. For each of them, it was like having thirteen brothers and sisters to sleep in a big warm pile with. And what could be better than thirteen brothers and sisters?

"As it happens, Mr. and Mrs. Davis," the attendant said, "four of our puppies are half border collie. Their father is a registered border collie named Joss and the mother is a shepherd mix, one of your typical mongrels—a good pet, gentle, and she loves children."

"We don't have children," Mister said.

"But we have friends who do," Missus said.

The attendant went on, "The three black-and-white males are from that litter, and there is one female. She's the sorrel—that reddish brown one with a cast on her rear leg. Take a look. You can tell the border collies by their coats and their ears and the way they stare. Border collies really stare, and right at you." The attendant looked at his clipboard. "Let me tell you about the shots the puppies have had, and we also require you to have them neutered or spayed." He held out a piece of paper.

But Mister and Missus had stopped paying attention to the attendant and started paying attention to the puppies.

They walked over to the pen and leaned over the wire to get closer. When the puppies caught sight of Mister and Missus, all fourteen of them rushed to greet them, from the biggest (one of the three male part border collies) to the smallest (the little reddish brown female border collie mix, who had a white nose, white paws, and a no-longer-white cast on one rear leg). The puppies ran as fast as they could up to the fence, stumbling over their own feet and one another's feet, too. They rushed to push their noses above the fence and smell the excitement.

Hello! Hello! Hello! They jumped up against the fence and fell down on top of one another. *Pet me! Pick me up!* They yipped and wagged their tails. *Me! Me!*

The little sorrel puppy tried to crawl up onto the pile near Missus, but her heavy cast held her back. She tried to burrow underneath, but the other puppies were crowded too tightly together. So she went around to the side and yipped. *Me! Me!* But when Missus tried to reach down to her, the pile of puppies rushed after her hand—and knocked the little white-and-sorrel puppy over onto her back. She lay there, her tail wagging fast.

"Oh dear," Missus said, but she was laughing.

"What's wrong with her leg?"

The puppy struggled over onto her three good legs and lumbered back toward Missus's hand. *Me!*

"She took a tumble down a steep set of cellar stairs, when she was only four or five weeks old, and broke it," the attendant answered. "She never got it set, so it healed wrong and so we had to rebreak it and reset it. Well, the surgeon had to. But it should be entirely mended in just a couple of weeks. Puppies are like babies, they heal quickly. And she doesn't mind it."

"I think she minds," Missus said. Her hand finally reached the puppy and the puppy snuggled up against it. *Yes, nice,* and she licked the fingers. *Mine.* Missus picked the puppy up, and the puppy tried to lick under her chin.

Meanwhile, Mister also put his hand down into the squiggling pile of puppies. He was reaching for the biggest one, who was mostly black, and that puppy had no trouble pushing his way straight to Mister's hand.

"Good boy," Mister said.

Me! The big black-and-white puppy planted his rear legs on the back of another puppy and pushed, jumping to get to Mister's hand. The other puppy tumbled over sideways into a third, and that third puppy growled and nipped at its own paw, as if it were the paw that had attacked him. Other puppies rushed to join in.

But the big black-and-white puppy did not let

himself get distracted. He took hold of Mister's hand with his teeth and pulled. *Me.*

Like all puppies, he had sharp, sharp teeth. As if he'd accidentally stuck his fingers into a box of needles, Mister jerked back his hand and flicked a finger at the wet black nose. "No!" he said, in a deep, stern voice.

The puppy closed its mouth, but he didn't back away. This time he butted his head up against the hand, instead of grabbing it. *Me.*

"You're a smart fellow, aren't you?" Mister asked, scratching the puppy behind the ears. "And big. How strong are you?" He picked the puppy up.

Yes, good. The black-and-white puppy licked Mister under the chin. *Mine.*

Now Mister and Missus stood facing one another. Each held a puppy. The little white-and-sorrel puppy

with the cast poked her nose up against Missus's neck and licked. It tickled, and Missus laughed. "This one," she said. "She's sweet. Affectionate."

"This one's a male, and bigger. And he's smart," Mister said. He and the black-and-white puppy both stared right at Missus.

Missus stared right back at the black puppy. "How do you know he's smart?" She reached her free hand over for him to smell, and he snuffled at her palm, his tail wagging fast.

Mine, too. Nice.

Missus scratched under his ear with one finger. "I don't care about bigger," she said. "But stronger would matter."

Mister looked at the little white-and-sorrel puppy, but she didn't notice him, not until he patted her on the head and rubbed one of her ears between his fingers, pulling it gently.

Oh—what? Nice. She squirmed to get closer to Mister's big hand.

"That is the sorriest looking dog I've seen in a long time," Mister said, and he laughed. "She must be the runt, and with that leg she's going to need special care."

"In another two or three weeks she'll be as good as new. But yours, you could start training pretty soon, couldn't you?"

Mister asked the attendant, "How old are they?"

"Eleven weeks. You can start training dogs at about, oh, three, three-and-a-half months."

"It seems so young," Missus said. There was too much talking and not enough petting, so the little sorrel puppy wriggled in her arms, trying to squirm up closer to her chin and lick it. "Are they housebroken?"

"Pretty much," the attendant said. "I meant you can train them to come, sit, and stay. You don't want a dog that's not trained," he told them.

"But why are they here, being given away?" Missus asked, stroking the puppy's bony head to keep her quiet.

"Well," the attendant answered. "Actually. A neighbor reported that they weren't being properly cared for. I mean, that leg was just neglected," he said. "The puppies were being neglected."

"Oh," Missus said.

"Good thing you're here to help the animals out," Mister said.

"Yes, I know," the attendant agreed.

"So, which one do you want?" Mister asked Missus.

"Which one do you?"

Mister didn't set the black-and-white puppy back down among the others, and Missus kept the white-and-sorrel close against her chest.

"I don't know," Mister said.

Take me. Take me.

"I can't decide," Missus said.

"We said only one," Mister said.

Take me. Take me.

"Although, if there were two, they could be friends," Missus said. "Do they get along all right?" she asked the attendant.

"Of course they do. They're siblings, littermates," the attendant said. "They've always been together."

Me.

Me.

"We only need one dog," Missus said.

"Just because we only need one doesn't mean we can't want two," Mister said. "And it doesn't mean we can't have two, either." He scratched with his fingers on the top of the black-and-white puppy's head.

Mine. Good.

"It's not as if we don't have room for two on the farm," Missus agreed, and she stroked the soft back of the white-and-sorrel puppy, all the way from her neck to the end of her tail.

Nice. Good. Yes.

"You have a farm?" the attendant asked. "Then you're perfect for these dogs."

So both puppies went home in the pickup truck with Mister and Missus, riding in a cardboard box behind the seat. It was strange to be in a box. They'd never been in a box before. They didn't know what to do. They didn't know what would happen, and the truck was so loud, it made them unhappy, uneasy. The little sorrel puppy climbed up on the big black-and-white one, and they both went to sleep.

By evening, they had been given their names. The black-and-white one was Angus, because he looked as if he might grow up to be as big and strong as a Black Angus bull. Angus was easy to name, but Mister and Missus disagreed about the little puppy. "Sorrel, for her color," Missus suggested. They were all sitting together on the kitchen floor.

"Just look at the sorry, lopsided way she walks," Mister said, and held out his fingers for the puppy to lick. "And the sorry way she doesn't even care what a sorry sight she is. We should call her Sorry."

"That's a terrible name. You can't call her that. The cast is going to come off and then she'll be just fine, not a sorry specimen at all—not that I think she's sorry now. I think she's sweet. How about a flower? How about Daisy or Rosie?"

"But she's funny-looking—the way her ear is half-flopped down, and the splotches of color over her eyes, like some masked avenger. You can't name her after a flower. That would be a joke."

"Sadie," said Missus unexpectedly.

"What?"

"Sadie, like Sadie Hawkins, in the old comic strip. Sadie Hawkins Day is named after her, because she was so homely—not that I think you're funny-looking, not a bit—nobody in Dogpatch would ask her to marry him. So there was one day a year when, if she could catch a man, he had to marry her."

Mister and the black-and-white puppy just stared at her, but the little sorrel puppy climbed up onto Missus's lap, to nuzzle up against her hands.

"Sadie's a good, old-fashioned name," Missus concluded.

"Sadie," Mister said, practicing it. "Sadie?" he asked, reaching his hand out to the little puppy.

Angus followed the hand. *Mine.*

The sorrel puppy stumbled toward Mister to reach his hand. He scratched her under the chin, and she licked him on the palm. "Sadie she is," he said.

"Angus and Sadie," Missus said. "That's settled. But now we'd better feed and walk them, so they have a chance to go to the bathroom and not have an accident during the night."

Mister stood up. "What do you say to some supper, Angus? Sadie?"

Me! Me!

Me, too!

The puppies didn't know what supper was, but they tried to climb up Mister's legs. "That's right," he said, and rubbed both of their heads.

Right!

Right!

"Do you think they're hungry?" Missus asked.

"They get fed three times a day while they're this little," Mister answered, "so they must be."

"It's lucky we got a big bag of puppy food." Missus took three metal mixing bowls down from the shelf and walked over to the kitchen door. "Angus and Sadie!" she called.

Angus and Sadie! they both answered, but neither left Mister's side.

"Let's go!" said Mister, moving across the kitchen.

Let's go!

Me first!

Missus poured brown crunchy bites into two metal bowls and set them down on the porch. She had already filled a third big bowl with water.

Food!

Let's go!

Angus went to one bowl and Sadie went to the other, but almost immediately Angus moved over to eat what

13

Sadie had. He pushed his head into her bowl, and nudged her head aside.

Sadie pushed her head right back in. With their heads crowded together, they ate until all of the brown bits were gone. Then Angus went back to the other bowl. Sadie followed him and pushed her head in beside his, so she could eat, too.

Mister and Missus stood and watched this and laughed.

After they finished eating, both dogs stuck a paw and their noses into the water and lapped it up with their tongues.

"I hope they're going to get a little neater with their eating," said Mister.

"I hope Sadie's getting enough," said Missus.

Then Mister said, "Let's go!" and he walked down the porch steps. Missus picked Sadie up, carried her down the stairs, and set her carefully on the ground. Angus ran after them, but the floor disappeared out from under him, and he tumbled down all three steps.

As soon as he hit the ground, Angus got up, shook himself, and stared at those steps. He stepped up onto the first one, and that was easy. So he went up to the top again, and then—more carefully this time—came down, front paws first, rear paws next, thump; front paws, rear paws, thump; and a final thump onto the ground. Now he knew. He guessed those steps wouldn't fool him again.

"This way," Missus said. "Let's go all the way around the house, out around the vegetable garden, and then down to the barn. They can start to learn where everything is."

There was still some daylight left in the air, and also some light coming from the porch. The puppies trailed after Mister and Missus, their noses down on the wet, muddy ground and in the wet grass. They were smelling everything. Some smells they already recognized, the Mister smell and the Missus smell and the watery, grassy, dirty smell. But everything else was new, and some of it was strong. Angus ran back and forth, smelling, while Sadie hobbled back and forth after him. He stopped, crouched, and peed. That reminded Sadie, who did the same.

"Good dogs, good," said Mister.

"Good Angus and Sadie," said Missus. "Good dogs."

Mine.

Mine, too.

They all walked together down a muddy path to a big, dark building with a big, dark doorway. "I'll get the light," Mister said, and suddenly the building was bright inside.

"Should we leave it on for them?" Missus wondered. "The barn can be pretty dark at night."

"They need to get used to it. They'll be fine. They have a blanket and water."

With the light on, the puppies ran into the barn. But something moved and they stopped. The something was big and it made a loud noise when it moved, so they ran out again.

"It's all right." Mister knelt down and held out his hand. "Come here, Angus. You, too, Sadie, everything's all right." Angus and Sadie both came up to be petted. Then Sadie ran over to Missus to be petted, and Angus followed, to push Sadie out of the way.

"It's only Bethie and she's in her stall, with Annie." Missus picked Angus up in her arms and carried him

over to where the sounds came from. "Bethie, Annie, this is Angus," she said to the big animals inside the dark box.

"And Sadie," said Mister, holding Sadie.

Smells good.

Mine.

Animals!

But not dogs.

Then Mister and Missus carried the puppies across the barn to the opposite side, past something bigger than the Bethie and Annie animals. But this wasn't an animal, and it didn't smell good. It had a nasty strong smell that a dog would never want to eat. Angus yipped at it from his safe place in Missus's arms. *Get away!*

Sadie buried her head under Mister's shoulder.

"It's only the tractor," Missus said. "It won't hurt you."

"It could," Mister told her.

"Not when it's in the barn and turned off," she said.

Beyond the tractor was another big stall. "This is your bedroom," Mister said, as he pulled open the half door and set Sadie down. Missus set Angus down beside Sadie. Mister and Missus closed the door, but they remained, leaning over the wall to see what the puppies did.

The stall was like a pen, only it didn't have wire walls you could see through. It had the same kind of animal smell that the Bethie and the Annie had, only faint and faded. The floor was covered with straw, and a blanket had been set in one corner, with a bowl of water nearby. The puppies ran all around the stall, smelling everything.

We have water!

I drank!

Me, too!

This is soft! Come here!

Soft!

"They're going to spill the water. They'll get water all over their blanket," Missus said. "Slow down," she called. "Take it easy."

Both puppies ran over to where she stood, and jumped up, trying to reach Mister and Missus.

"We're just getting them overexcited," Mister said. "We should leave. Good night, Angus and Sadie. Welcome home."

"They're so little. Do you think they'll be all right in here?"

"Why not? There are only the cows."

Cows?

The Bethie?

The Annie, too?

"You forgot the cats," Missus said. "Those cats are half wild."

Cats?

The Annie and the Bethie?

"The puppies are going to have to learn how to get along here, with the cats and the cows, and with us, too. Angus is smart and strong. He can take care of himself."

"But Sadie," Missus said, sounding doubtful. Then she smiled, and reached down to stroke Sadie's head. "She's so sweet—who could be mean to her? You'll take care of her, won't you, Angus?" and she stroked his head, too.

Mister reached down to give Angus and Sadie a final pat, and then he and Missus just looked down at the two puppies.

Angus and Sadie stared back up at them and wagged their tails.

"They don't look much alike," Missus said.

"They don't act much alike," Mister said.

"Do you think they'll get along with each other?"

"I hope so," Mister said, "because they don't have any choice about it."

Mister and Missus went away. Angus and Sadie listened to their footsteps. Then the lights went out.

Dark!

Uh-oh!

Listen!

Noises moved around the dark barn, and not all of

them came from the Bethie and the Annie, who might be cows but might also be cats. Sadie curled up next to Angus because he was warm, and he curled up next to her. They fell asleep, tired out by the day, so deeply asleep that they didn't even stir when the two barn cats crept in to examine them.

2

How Angus and Sadie get in trouble
and learn their way around,
and how Angus is a hero

As soon as they heard the big barn door sliding open the next morning, the puppies awoke and started to feel hungry. They were ready to get out of that stall.

"Good morning, Angus, and good morning, Sadie," said Mister, opening their stall door. "It's good to see you. Sleep well? Ah, I see you did knock over your water."

They ran up to him, as he bent down to pet them.

Good.

Mine.

"Listen up now, you two. We have a routine to

establish. I know you need a routine," Mister said. "First, we let Bethie and Annie out, because they need attention first thing in the morning."

The puppies followed him after their own little side trip to smell the stalls where the Bethie and the Annie were shuffling their feet and making low sounds and to see if the tractor smelled any better. Whenever the puppies started heading off in their own direction, Mister called, "Angus and Sadie, stick with me. Come."

When they came out into the cool, brightening morning air, Angus went running off around the side of the barn. *What's this? What's there?*

Me, too, said Sadie, following as fast as she could, although her cast kept that from being very fast.

"No! Stop! Come! Angus and Sadie!" called Mister, running along behind.

Angus did stop, because there was a fence with wooden railings and wires. He stopped, and then crawled under it. There was a smell of an unknown animal. All of the mud had that animal smell.

What? He wondered, smelling the railings.

Sadie was trying to get her cast under the fence.

Mister came up and said, "Come on, you two. Come with me." He held out his hand to them, and there was food in it.

Hungry!

Me, too!

When they got back to the driveway, they heard Missus calling, "Angus and Sadie, breakfast," in a voice that made them want to run up to her. So they did, and Mister walked behind.

"Where did you go?" asked Missus.

"They discovered the sheep pen," Mister reported. "It's a good thing the sheep aren't still there."

Sheep, Angus told Sadie. *That smell is sheep.*

Smell that! she answered.

There was a smell of food in the air. Angus went right up the stairs, but Sadie needed to be carried and set down at the top.

This time, there was only one big bowl filled with brown bits. They put their faces into that bowl and ate fast, until the bowl was empty.

"How long will it take them to learn their names? And what are we going to do with them all day?" Missus asked.

"I think we just have to let them be puppies for a couple of weeks. They'll amuse themselves."

"What if they run away?" Missus asked.

"Why should they run away?" Mister asked. "We're here. Food's here. They'll stick together. And Sadie can't go far, or fast. You'll see. We'll keep them close to us for a day or two, and by then they'll be used to everything."

"I'm putting a bucket of water and some rags out here, so we can wash off their paws before they come in the house," Missus said. "It's mud season, you know."

"In Maine, we call that spring," said Mister.

Angus and Sadie quickly learned that their food was put out on the porch in the morning, at midday, and in the evening. Because of Sadie's cast, their water bowl stayed down at the bottom of the steps. After a day, they had learned how to find their way back to the house—and the barn, too, from anywhere on the farm.

They learned that if they ran around behind the barn and got lost, they could run across the sheep pen to get to the vegetable garden. They also learned that it was not good to run into the Bethie and the Annie, thump!

When they did that, Mister ran out to say, "Angus and Sadie! Stop that! Leave the cows alone!"

So they learned what the cows were. They learned that it also wasn't good to run yipping all around the chicken cage, and make the chickens gabble and squawk and flutter up into the air, scurrying back into their little house. Missus would come running to say sternly, "Angus and Sadie, you stop that right now! Leave the chickens alone."

Most of what the puppies learned in those first days getting used to the farm was what got them into trouble. It was bad to drink from the pails of milk Mister got from the cows every morning. That was very bad, very very bad, and if the puppies did that they would get a smack on the rump, both of them. Also very bad was to grab two corners of the seed trays Missus had set out on a low table, and pull as hard as you could, twisting your heads, pulling, until the dirt all spilled out and the tray broke, and you had to go get another one to play with. When the puppies did that, Missus came out with her broom and she swept at them. Worse than that, she didn't want them close to her while she picked up the trays and the little tomato and pepper seedlings. She didn't want to talk to them either.

Some other things that got the puppies into trouble were taking a boot from beside the doorway and carrying it down the steps to play keep-away with, bringing a whisk broom out from the barn and chewing on it until it was all crumbled away, climbing up into the tall bin in the kitchen where Missus sometimes hid food in a lot of paper, and taking the squares of cloth Missus kept in her quilting basket in the living room for a game of tug-of-war.

The puppies also learned that it was good to keep still while their paws were being rinsed off and dried before they went into the house. It was good to run around after each other inside the house and to stand looking out the windows together. It was good to chew on sticks of wood from the pile beside the fire, although you got in trouble if you chewed on the legs of the kitchen chairs.

"Those puppies need some toys," Missus decided, and she took the pickup into town. She came back with special toys that made squeaky noises when the puppies bit on them. She kept some of the toys in the kitchen, but she also put one for Angus and one for Sadie in their stall in the barn. When Sadie woke up alone at night she chewed gently on it, and it squeaked to tell her everything was all right. Angus was happy to have his in the stall, because he needed some time to work on it, to find out what that squeaker was. In the morning, after he had done that, and fixed it so it would never squeak again, he took Sadie's.

Mine, he said. *I need it.*

All right, and she ran her head right into his shoulder, so that he turned—dropping the toy—and tried to chew on her hip. That knocked her over. *Play!*

Play, yes!

They called it playing, but Mister and Missus called it wrestling and wouldn't let them do it inside the house. "Angus and Sadie, stop that wrestling around. If you have to wrestle, you better go outside," Missus said, and she held the kitchen door open.

All right.

Let's go!

Not down the stairs.

Yes, you can.

So Sadie learned how to clump and stumble down the porch steps to the yard, where they could play without getting into trouble.

It didn't take the puppies long to learn about the farm and where everybody on it belonged. Mister and Missus belonged everywhere, anywhere they wanted to go in the house and the fields and the barn. Bethie and Annie belonged in the barn and in their pasture, where the stream ran. The absent sheep belonged in their pen behind the barn and also in a little warm room next to the kitchen, which Mister called the lambing room, and Missus called the dairy room because she made butter there.

The chickens had their cage, with its own little low house. Patches stayed in the farmhouse, going anywhere he wanted inside, and sometimes out onto the porch, if there was sun. The puppies belonged wherever Mister and Missus went.

The puppies liked every day on the farm, and Mister and Missus liked them, too, every day. The only bad things about the farm were the barn cats.

The barn cats did not welcome Angus and Sadie, and they did not plan to get used to them. The barn cats didn't get along with anyone, and they were proud of it. They had their own lives to live. They couldn't be bothered with puppies. They weren't one bit afraid of dogs, either. In fact, Sadie was afraid of them. They knew that—and they enjoyed it. If it was a cold and rainy day and the barn cats were hungry, or if it was a fine day and they were full but they were bored—one of them would smack Sadie across the nose or grab her tail to make her yelp. The cat would attack, Sadie would yelp and run away, and the cat would feel better.

Call me Fox, the white barn cat said to Sadie.

But you're not a fox, Sadie said.

Oh yeah? And my friend's Snake, and those are our own names.

All right, Sadie said. She guessed everybody could have her own name.

Fox was the bigger of the barn cats, and the meaner. Sometimes, in the dark of night, she jumped up onto the door of their stall so she could leap down on Sadie, letting out a long, lovely, high shriek as she descended. When Fox fell shrieking onto Sadie, Sadie woke up yelping, and that woke up Angus. He barked his loudest, but by then Fox would have run off, entirely satisfied, while Sadie was trying to tunnel under the blanket to safety.

In the daytime, if Angus was there with Sadie, the cats lifted their noses and yawned. *We can't be bothered with puppies*, they said. *Don't think we're afraid of anything like a puppy.*

Oh yeah? Angus asked, staring right at them with his fixed unwavering border collie stare. *Oh yeah?*

The cats would walk away, tails high, noses in the air. *We have something important to do over there, or we'd show you what's what.*

For the first couple of weeks, Angus and Sadie were always together, in the house with Missus while she cooked or in the garden with her when she checked on the seedlings in her planting trays. They went together to the barn with Mister as he took apart the tractor engine and polished the pieces. They explored the gardens and pastures together, getting wet in the stream and muddy in the sheep pen. They took naps together and they slept together at night, in their stall in the barn. They chased each other's tails and wrestled.

"Poor Sadie is always getting the worst of it," said Missus. "Angus is always starting fights and he always wins."

"I don't know about that," said Mister.

"Don't know about the starting or the winning? Because it's always Angus standing over Sadie at the end."

Just then Angus and Sadie came racing around the barn, Angus far in the lead. He stopped when he saw Fox standing in the barn doorway. When he stopped, Sadie caught up with him, and she bit at his ears to pull him over. He bit at her muzzle until their mouths were locked, and then she pushed at him with her head. But her cast kept her clumsy and off-balance, so she was the one who fell over. Angus jumped to stand over her and keep her on her back.

I win.

Play!

"I guess you're right," said Missus. "I guess maybe she likes wrestling."

Angus jumped off and Sadie jumped up, and he grabbed her by the tail.

"They're getting bigger fast," said Mister.

Sadie grabbed Angus by his tail, and they chased themselves in a circle until they both fell over.

"Angus and Sadie!" called Missus. "What are you two doing?"

I'm Angus, said Angus. *Just Angus.*
All right.
And you're just Sadie.
I know.
And *doesn't count,* said Angus.

After that first couple of weeks, Mister and Missus decided it was time for the puppies to be apart sometimes. Mister took Angus with him to work at clearing out the winter treefalls in the woods. As long as Sadie had her cast, they thought she would be better off at home with Missus. "She can't walk far," Mister said.

Sadie couldn't go as far as Angus, but she did walk almost every day with Missus, down the long driveway to the mailbox, after the lunch dishes were washed and Mister and Angus had returned to their work. Missus took a leash from the hook by the kitchen door and called, "Let's go, Sadie!" Sadie came thumping onto the porch and down the steps, keeping right in front of Missus, and they set off.

The long driveway smelled of warm sunny dirt and of the pickup tires; after a rain its puddles tasted of mud. Ditches lay on both sides. Even with the cast on her leg, Sadie could get down into the ditch to smell everything there and bring Missus back a nice stone or chunk of grass. At the last curve before they came to the road,

Sadie had to stop so Missus could clip the leash onto her collar. "We can't have you going out into the road, can we? And we certainly don't want you to even *think* about chasing cars." Missus and Sadie walked the last section of driveway together. Then, after Missus emptied out the mailbox, they turned around to walk back up the driveway, back home.

Once they had rounded the curve again, Missus unclipped the leash. "Go ahead, girl, explore. See what you can see, like the bear who went over the mountain. Do you know about that bear, Sadie?"

Don't know bear. Don't know mountain. But I know ditch. This is the ditch!

"Now where are you going? You're the silliest, sorriest dog I've ever seen," Missus said. "Sorriest, silliest, sweetest . . . sportiest? No. Not sportiest. You're not a bit sporty, are you?"

Sporty, yes!

Missus liked to talk, no matter what she was doing. "All right, Sadie. We've finished the kitchen and the bed is made," Missus would say in the morning. "Now's our chance to get out in the garden. It's finally spring, Sadie. It's almost time to plant. Isn't it a beautiful day?"

Let's go!

At first, Missus worked in the garden with a rototiller. "We're getting the soil ready," she explained. "Turning it over, aerating it, mixing in manure."

Sadie kept away from the rototiller. It was a machine like the tractor, loud and smelly and scary. Angus had explained it to her: *Stay away from machines. Unless it's the pickup, of course.* When Missus turned on the rototiller, Sadie ran over to the porch and hid behind the steps. She would have done that even without the warning from Angus. A machine sounded like something that would like to crunch you up.

Missus agreed with her. "Good move, Sadie. You're getting smarter every day, as well as bigger."

Yes, smarter!

But the rototiller came out only for the first two days Missus worked in the garden. After that, she used a shovel, and after that, the hoe and pitchfork, so Sadie could dig right alongside of her, helping. While Sadie and Missus gardened, Patches sat in the kitchen window or curled up in a puddle of sunlight on the porch, to watch and sleep.

When Angus was off working with Mister, Patches and Sadie took naps together on the rug in front of the kitchen sink, or stretched out nose-to-nose behind one of the rocking chairs on the porch. Sometimes Sadie chased Patches around the house, barking at him, and sometimes Patches pretended to be trying to catch Sadie by the tail.

You can't be friends with a cat, Angus told Sadie.

All right, Sadie said, but she napped and played with Patches all the same. If Angus said they couldn't be friends, he was probably right; but Sadie went on liking Patches even if they weren't friends. The friend question puzzled her. *Am I your friend?* she asked Angus. *Are we friends?*

Of course, he told her. *We're dogs. Dogs are always friends with other dogs. Unless it's a dog you don't know, from another farm, and he wants to come onto your farm. Or unless you don't like them.*

I'll probably like them, Sadie said.

You better be careful about who you like, Angus warned her.

All right, Sadie said.

As long as Sadie had the cast on her leg, Angus had Mister all to himself all day long. They walked across the grassy pastures together, with Angus on a leash, to check the winter damage to the fences that kept the cows and sheep safe. They checked the wooden railings and the electric fence wires. They rode the tractor, with Mister lifting Angus up into the cab before they started off to plow the fields.

They rode the tractor on a dirt road into the woods, and then climbed together over low stone fences, walking right into the woods. Mister let Angus run free while he cut up fallen trees with his chainsaw. Angus quickly got used to the roar of the tractor as it turned over the soil in the fields or pulled a flatbed into the woods to be loaded with logs. He even got used to the whine of the chainsaw as it cut through trees, lopping off branches, slicing up trunks.

"Stand back!" Mister called, when a machine started up. When Mister said that, Angus backed away to a safe distance from the noise. "Clever boy," Mister said. Then Angus lay down, waiting until the job was done, keeping an eye on Mister the whole time. "Good dog," Mister said.

At the end of the day, when Mister and Angus came home for supper, they all stayed in the kitchen together. Mister and Missus sat at the table, eating. Angus and Sadie had already eaten, so they stretched out on the floor near the warmth of the stove to rest. Patches sat on the windowsill, among pots of aloe and parsley, rosemary, mint, and a cyclamen with bright white flowers. "I like flowers in my kitchen," Missus said, "even if they are useless. I like flowers in my life."

Angus told Sadie about all the things he had seen and done that day, after which he dozed off for a little nap. Sadie wasn't tired, but she took a nap, too. Patches kept his distance, up on the deep windowsill behind the sink. Whenever Angus was around, Patches preferred to keep his distance.

After they finished in the kitchen, the dogs took a bathroom walk outside. After they went back inside, Missus combed and brushed them, telling them how handsome they were. Then Mister walked down to the barn with Angus at his side and Sadie lolloping behind. Sometimes Missus came with them and sometimes not. Angus led the way into their stall, and Sadie followed. Mister no longer closed the stall door. Now he just said,

"Keep an ear out. It's up to you, Angus." They heard him say, "Good night, ladies," to Bethie and Annie before he left the barn, closing the big doors behind him. Then, they heard his faint steps as he walked back up along the path to the house.

You can't go to sleep yet, Angus told Sadie.

All right.

We have to listen. When we know everything is okay, then we can go to sleep.

Everything is okay, Sadie said. She could hear that. The restless barn cats were padding around the loft. The cows shuffled in the hay, and the tractor smelled nasty, just the way it was supposed to. *You can sleep. I can sleep.*

Something bad could happen.

If something bad happens, we'll wake up and you'll fix it, Sadie answered. She lay down to go to sleep, curled up against Angus's warm body. Angus stayed awake and listened, and listened, for a long time. Then he went to sleep, too.

Soon the puppies had lived on the farm long enough to have forgotten they had ever lived anywhere else, and long enough for spring to have pulled bright green leaves out from the trees and pushed soft green seedlings up in the garden. One spring day, Angus and Mister took the tractor into the woods and then climbed down to walk

along a dirt road, looking for fallen trees to clear away. Mister carried his chainsaw and Angus was off the leash. The soft mossy ground under their feet smelled of unknown animal tracks, but Angus didn't feel like exploring that day. He felt like sticking close to Mister, following right behind Mister's boots, stopping when Mister stopped to examine a fallen tree, waiting while Mister sawed it into pieces and put them into neat piles. They had gotten deep into the woods when Angus heard—far away—a high noise. He had never heard anything like that before, but as soon as he heard it he knew something was wrong. Angus ran to see what was happening. He barked to tell Mister, *Trouble! Follow me!*

Mister yelled and chased after him, but Angus was much faster than Mister, especially in the woods, where he could run low to the ground and Mister had to crash through, carrying the heavy chainsaw. Running fast and low, Angus left Mister far behind.

At last, Angus found the noise. It came from an animal that smelled like the pen behind the barn, so he knew it must be a sheep. The sheep had fallen down into a steep gulley and gotten tangled in some bushes at the bottom. She was thrashing with her legs, trying to get free, trying to stand up, making high bleating sounds.

What are you doing down there? Angus asked. *Get out of there! You better come back up!*

The sheep kicked its legs, bleating in fear and misery.

You have to get up.

Bleat! Bleat! The sheep struggled even harder, as if, instead of helping, Angus had just made her more frightened.

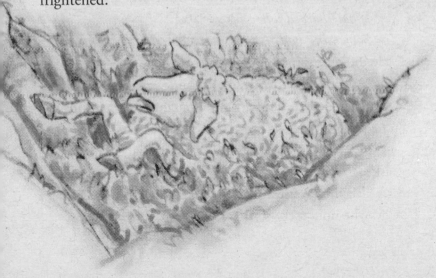

Angus didn't know what to do. But he was sure that Mister would understand what was wrong and fix it. Angus turned back the way he'd come and ran to find Mister.

Running from opposite directions, Angus and Mister almost crashed into each other. Mister demanded angrily, "What got into you, Angus? You're a bad—"

Then he heard the thrashing and bleating, and he lifted his head to listen. "What?" he asked. "What's that?" He set down the chainsaw and ran. "Come on!" he called, and Angus followed close behind him.

Later, Mister told Missus all about it while they were eating supper and the two dogs were lying in front of the oven. "The silly thing had got herself tangled up in vines and undergrowth."

"Good thing it wasn't barbed wire," Missus remarked.

What's barbed wire? asked Sadie.

Something bad, Angus answered. *It catches your legs.* He thought some more. *It hurts.*

"And every move the silly thing made just got her more tangled and more tightly caught," Mister said. "So she panicked. Well, sheep do that."

"Would you have found her if Angus hadn't?" Missus asked.

"Maybe." Mister paused and thought and then said, "Maybe not."

"Good dog, Angus," Missus said. "You're a smart one, aren't you?"

Yes. I am. Angus's tail thumped against the floor. He was feeling proud, and happy, too, because he had helped Mister.

"If Angus hadn't been there, the poor silly thing might well have died before I noticed she'd gone missing and went looking for her in the part of the woods where she'd gotten herself trapped. But Angus saved the day."

"He saved the sheep at least," Missus said, and they both laughed. "The day isn't over yet," she added, and they laughed again.

After he had eaten some more, Mister said, "You know what that means. There's a break in the fence around the spring pasture. I thought I was finished with fences for the year."

"You're never finished with fences on a farm," Missus answered.

You're smart, Sadie said to Angus.

And I did a good job of saving the sheep, Angus answered. He liked being the dog who saved the sheep. That was the only dog he wanted to be.

Am I smart?

Not as smart as me.

Maybe when I get my cast off, Sadie said.

Probably not, Angus told her. *But don't worry. I'm here to take care of you.*

"On the other hand," Mister said, "Angus didn't come back when I called him. He just kept on running away. It's time that dog had some training."

"What about Sadie?"

"It's time for both of them. They're more than three months old. Doesn't the cast come off next week? Shouldn't we make a couple of appointments at the vet's? We'll start training after that."

Did you hear? Sadie asked. *Did you hear that? I'll be able to run! I'll be able to run with you!*

I can run faster, Angus warned her. *I'm bigger, and stronger.*

I know, Sadie said. *But I won't have a cast! I'll be able to run! I'll be able to run with you!*

3

How both dogs visit the vet,
Angus is better at being trained,
and Sadie isn't a fetcher

They all went into town together to go to the vet. Angus and Sadie were too big now for their box, so they rode behind the seats, climbing back and forth, over and under each other, to look out the windows.

"Settle down, you two," Mister said.

They didn't know "settle down," but they understood his tone of voice. Mister didn't like what they were doing.

"They're just nervous," Missus said.

"They don't know enough to know to be nervous," Mister said.

"Maybe they do," Missus said. "How do we know what they know?"

As soon as they entered the vet's office, Angus and Sadie were suspicious. There was something about it they didn't like. It smelled bad in a nasty, sharp, clean way, and the floor was slippery. It wasn't the farm. It wasn't home.

"It's going to be all right, I promise," Missus told Angus. "Dr. Anderson is a very good vet, and you'll have Sadie for company."

"You'll both be back home tomorrow," Mister told Sadie. "You'll have Angus for company."

They could tell that Mister and Missus were worried, too.

What's going to happen? Sadie asked.

It'll be all right. Missus said.

What will be all right?

We'll be home tomorrow.

When's tomorrow?

Angus wasn't sure. *Soon.* He was too worried to want to talk anymore. *Very soon.*

As it turned out, Angus was correct. But before tomorrow came, they all went together into a bright little room to meet the vet, a man in a white coat, who crouched down to stroke their whole bodies, and look at their mouths, and pull gently on their ears. It wasn't petting, but it was nice. "They look grand, Mr. Davis," he said to Mister. "Are they eating well? Are they lively enough?"

"More than lively enough," said Missus.

"Well, they would be. They're part border collie," the vet said. "You can leave them here with me, now. We'll do everything—shots, cast off—while they're unconscious. That'll be the easiest for them. Come back anytime after seven in the morning. Somebody's always here by seven. They'll be ready."

While the vet was talking, Angus stuck close to Mister's leg and Sadie stuck close to Missus.

I want to go home.

Me, too.

"I'm not too happy about leaving them," Missus said.

"Not to worry. This is just routine," the doctor said.

Routine, said Angus. *It's just routine. Everything's going to be fine.*

All right, Sadie said.

Mister and Missus gave the doctor the leashes and let him lead them away, and it turned out that Angus was right again because when the doctor talked to them, they fell asleep, and when they woke up they only wanted to go back to sleep again, so they did. Then Mister and Missus were there to take them home.

In the truck, Missus said, "I bought you new collars, because you're bigger now. Red for Angus and green for Sadie."

I feel wrong. Bad.

Me, too.

"They're color-blind. They don't care what colors they wear."

We should go to sleep.

All right.

When the truck stopped, and the dogs were lifted out, for a minute they were so glad to be home that they felt fine. Missus put the new collars on them. "You both look very handsome," she said, and she petted them both on the head and the ears. "And, see? You have name tags, too, so you can't get lost."

Home!

Look! I have my own leg!

"Name tags won't keep them from getting lost," Mister told her.

"You know what I mean," Missus said. "I mean, anybody who finds them will know they belong here, with us."

"If they get lost around here, they're more likely to get found by coyotes or bobcats than people," Mister said. "That's why it's important for them to learn to come when we call them, and stay when we tell them to." At the vet's Mister had bought a choke chain collar and a book for dog training.

Look at me! The cast is gone!

Sadie tried to run over to play with Angus, but her leg felt funny now. It felt as if it didn't know what it was doing. She took off toward the garden, and then turned right—and that leg didn't know how to turn. So she fell down. She scrambled up and tried again, more slowly.

I feel bad, she realized. *Not my leg.*

I feel worse than you, Angus said. *We should go to sleep. All right.*

They lay down together in the grass by the porch steps, where the sun could warm them and the barn cats would leave them alone.

A few days later, when the dogs felt normal and good again, and Sadie had gotten so used to having four legs the same that she almost forgot she had ever had a cast on one, training began. After breakfast, before the day's work, Mister and Missus took the dogs out to the grassy lawn in front of the barn. They had both read the training book, so they knew both masters had to train both dogs.

"Only a few minutes at first," Mister reminded Missus.

"I read the book, too," she reminded him.

"I'll go first, then you," he told her.

"We start with Sit," she told him.

Mister removed Angus's red collar and replaced it with the choke chain collar. Then he clipped on a leash.

Missus and Sadie sat together on the grass, and watched.

Angus looked right at Mister, and waited.

"Angus, Sit!" Mister said.

What?

"Sit!" Mister said again.

Angus stared right at Mister, waiting to understand.

Mister pulled up hard on the leash.

What? The chain closed tight around Angus's throat. *What? What!* Angus stuck his muzzle up into the air, trying to loosen the collar, and that lifted his whole head up, which lifted his shoulders up. All that lifting made his haunches go lower and lower, until he had his rear end down on the ground with his nose still pointing high into the air. "Good dog," Mister said, and then he lowered the leash and the collar was comfortable again.

"Good dog," Mister said again. He bent over and rubbed Angus on the shoulder. "Good dog, good boy."

Angus stood up and shook himself; he was good, everything was all right. He licked Mister's hand.

Mister stood up, too, but instead of walking off to get to work, he said, "Angus, Sit!"

What? Again? But—

Before Angus could even start to wonder, Mister jerked up on the leash and the chain tightened. Immediately, without even thinking, Angus lifted his nose and lowered his rear. Then Mister bent down and praised him again. "Good, good dog. Good boy." He scratched Angus behind the ears. "What a good dog."

This time Angus didn't lick Mister's hand. This time he stood up a little more slowly, and wagged his tail a little cautiously, because he wasn't sure what would happen next, although he thought he might be able to guess. And he was right.

"Angus, Sit!" Mister said.

Before Mister could pull up on the leash, before the choke chain collar could tighten around his neck, Angus put his rear on the ground. "All right!" Mister said, and he sounded excited. He crouched down in front of Angus, and pulled gently on his ears in the way Angus liked best. "Did you see how quickly he caught on?"

"I saw," Missus said. "But I have to say, I'm not sure Sadie was paying attention."

"Border collies are good learners," Mister said.

"Although she probably won't get it as quickly." He stood up then. Angus stood up, too, and waited in front of him, watching his face.

Mister took a couple of steps backward, still holding onto the leash, then said, "Angus, Sit!"

Suddenly, Angus really understood. He understood and he obeyed. He sat.

Mister was very excited. "What a good dog. What a smart dog. You are really something, Angus." He stroked and patted Angus, rubbing with both hands up and down the fur on Angus's shoulders. "You really are something."

They did Sit! two more times, and then Mister said, "That'll do!" Mister took the choke chain collar from around Angus's neck, and put the red collar back on. When his collar was back on and he had been praised and patted again, Angus barked for the excitement of it all.

Sadie barked, too, *Good boy!* as excited as Angus was. While Sadie barked, Angus ran around in a big circle, circling Mister and Missus and Sadie. *I'm smart! I'm good!*

Sadie got up to run around behind him. Because she was still getting used to not having a cast, Sadie stumbled—*Oops!*—and fell. She scrambled right up—*I slipped!*—and went back to running behind Angus. *Me, too! Smart and good, me, too!*

When she came close to Mister, his big hands reached

51

out and caught her by the shoulders.

What? Oh! Hello! Hello!

"Your turn, Sadie," Mister said. He took off her green collar and slipped the choke chain over her head.

Me, too! Just like Angus!

Mister clipped the leash to the choke chain collar. Sadie stood, watching his face while her tail wagged in excitement.

"Sadie, Sit!" Mister said.

Sadie stood and watched and waited.

"Sadie, Sit!" he said again, and at the same time his hand jerked into the air, pulling up hard on the leash.

Gaggh! The collar was choking her! She backed away from it, trying to get away, but it just choked her tighter. *No! No!*

Mister said something, but Sadie couldn't hear him. She tried to howl, but the collar was too tight to let the howl out. She had to get away! Missus said something, but Sadie couldn't hear that either. *Help!* She didn't even hear what Angus was saying, because all she could think about was fighting free of that collar.

Then Mister's hand came down lower, and she could breathe again.

"Take it easy, girl. Calm down. It's okay, everything's okay," he said. He stroked her, his hand running over her head, two strokes, three, four. "Calm down, easy now."

He pulled gently on her ears. "It's only training," he said, in a gentle voice.

It was terrible! Sadie said.

Just do what he tells you, Angus advised her.

I couldn't breathe!

It's training. When you do what he tells you the collar doesn't choke.

You don't understand. I couldn't breathe.

He wouldn't hurt us.

It did hurt!

"Better now?" Mister asked. "Ready to try again? This will be much easier."

Sadie had her doubts about that. *Maybe it will be different,* she hoped, now that Mister understood how much that collar had choked her.

But when Mister stood up and said, "Sadie, Sit!" and she didn't understand, his hand pulled up on the leash again and the collar choked her again, just like the first time. *No! Help! Stop!* When Sadie pulled harder and harder on the collar, backing away to get her head free, Mister lifted his hand higher and higher, until Sadie's paws were barely touching the ground. *Stop! No! Help! Help! Help!*

Mister's hand came down lower, and the collar loosened, and Sadie just stood there, breathing as fast as she could.

"All right," Mister said. "It's all right, Sadie."

"She's terrified," Missus said.

"I can see that," Mister said. "Sadie, that'll do!" he said, and took off the choke chain collar. As he buckled her own collar back around her neck he said, "We're going to have to go slowly with you, I can see that. But don't worry, you'll get it eventually."

I already got it, Angus said.

I don't want to get it, Sadie told him. She ran to Missus, climbed up into her lap, and buried her nose under Missus's arm.

"It's all right, Sadie," Missus said, stroking her back. "It's not as bad as it seems now. We wouldn't do anything bad to you, you know that."

It was bad.

"Your turn now," Mister said.

Missus put the collar on Angus, and told him, "Sit! Angus." Angus didn't know what she wanted, so he waited patiently for further instructions. "Angus, Sit!" she said again, and he waited some more. "Angus, Sit!" she said, and raised her arm, pulling on the choke chain collar.

Oh. Angus remembered now. *Is this what you want?*

"Good dog," Missus said, crouching down and petting him.

I know.

She asked Angus to sit twice more, and the first time he remembered perfectly, even if he didn't the second time. Then Missus put the choke chain collar on Sadie. "Don't worry," she said. "I won't pull hard."

Sadie tried not to worry.

"She's trembling," Missus said.

"Just try," Mister said.

"Sadie, Sit!" said Missus, and then she said it again, "Sadie, Sit!"

Sadie stood and shook and watched. She didn't think Missus would do anything terrible, but she wasn't sure.

"Sadie, Sit!" This time, Missus raised her arm. Sadie backed away and Missus lowered her arm. "It won't work. Isn't there any other way?" she asked. "I'm going to look at that chapter again. Sadie can't be the only dog ever to be spooked by a choke chain collar."

"If you want, go ahead and see," Mister said. "Right now, there's fertilizing to be done, isn't there, Angus?"

So while Angus and Mister left to do their work, Missus and Sadie went inside to do theirs, and everything was back to normal. Everything was fine.

After lunch, however, everything became not fine again, and it was worse because Sadie knew ahead of time how bad it was going to be. After lunch, after Angus had his training and was a good and clever dog again (once he remembered how to Sit!), Mister put the choke chain collar on Sadie. As soon as he clipped the leash to it, Sadie started to pull back to get away, until finally she lay flat on the ground, her head on her front paws. Her whole body shook. "For heaven's sake," Mister said, in a heavy loud voice. "Sadie—" But he didn't say Sit! He didn't say anything at all because he was busy not being angry. The book said never get angry, because having an angry trainer doesn't help a dog to learn. After a minute, Mister leaned down to loosen the collar around Sadie's neck and pat her on the head.

Sadie didn't move. She knew that as soon as she moved, the collar would choke her again.

"I don't know," Mister said, but he didn't say what he didn't know.

Sadie just stayed there flat on the ground, with her legs gathered up under her and her nose between her front paws. She kept her eyes closed. If her eyes stayed closed, she couldn't see Mister or the leash, and if she couldn't see them, it was the same as if they weren't there. Except for the choke chain collar, of course; she could still feel the weight of the choke chain collar, and it was the choke chain collar that made all the trouble.

Then Mister took the collar off and said, in not so heavy a voice, "That'll do! We'll try later. It won't be so bad once you get used to it, Sadie."

Later. Sadie agreed about that. She was happy now, with her own collar on and Mister stroking her head. She licked his hand. *Later.* She wasn't sure when later meant, but it wasn't now.

What is wrong with you? Angus asked her.

Nothing anymore. Why? Is something wrong with you? But Sadie knew there was never anything wrong with Angus. *When is later, do you know?*

Later turned out to be before they went inside for supper. Once again, Angus had forgotten how to Sit!, but he remembered when Mister reminded him, and he forgot and remembered again when Missus took her turn to train him. When Angus was finished, Mister said, "In a couple of days I'm going to try him on a longer lead. I bet it won't be long before there's no need for a choke chain collar at all." Mister's voice sounded happy. Sadie was happy, too, until Mister said, "Your turn now, Sadie," and held out the collar.

Sadie knew about that collar, and she didn't wait one minute. She took off. She ran across the grass and up the hillside, as fast as she could. She heard Angus barking. *Where are you going?* Mister ran after her, but he couldn't catch her, now that she didn't have her cast on. Without the cast, Sadie ran faster than any of them, except Angus.

She didn't go very far before Missus said, "Probably you shouldn't chase her."

Mister stopped running. "Then how do I catch her?"

As they were talking, Sadie stopped to see what would happen next. She stopped and watched, but she kept her distance.

"She's frightened of the collar," Missus said.

"I know that. But she needs it for training. Angus isn't frightened."

"Angus isn't Sadie." Missus got up. "Let me try something." She walked toward Sadie. "It's okay, Sadie," she said, coming closer, holding out her hand. "Come here," she said. Sadie ran up to her, and Missus bent over to stroke her on the head and down her neck, and to pull gently on her ear.

Good, nice.

Then Missus ran her hand all the way down Sadie's back and pushed down on her rear, saying, "Sadie, Sit!" in a clear, plain voice. She pushed down until Sadie sat on the ground, watching Missus carefully to see what she wanted, because that voice was one that wanted Sadie to pay attention, and to do something. "Good dog," Missus said.

Yes, me, too. Good dog.

Missus walked away a couple of steps, and Sadie came

along, too. Then Missus stopped and bent over to push down again, and to say in her plain voice, "Sadie, Sit!" When Sadie sat again, Missus patted her again and said, "Clever dog, very good, that's it exactly."

Clever me. Sadie liked being good and clever.

Again Missus moved and Sadie followed and Missus stopped. But this time Missus didn't bend over to pet or to push, she just said, "Sadie, Sit!" Sadie waited, watching, and in no time, Missus leaned over with her hand out to start pushing as she said, "Sit!"

Oh, Sit. Sadie sat. *Easy.* Sadie hoped she had figured out what it was Missus wanted her to do.

"Good girl," Missus said. "That'll do!" she said, and walked back to join Mister with Sadie running around her feet in circles. "See?"

"Yes, but will she remember?"

"Maybe not right away, but neither does Angus. It's repetition that helps them learn. It's practice, not the collar. How would you feel about not using the choke chain collar at all? The book said we should be consistent."

"Probably, Angus doesn't *need* it."

"I don't like the idea of choking a dog to get her to obey," Missus admitted.

"When you put it that way, I don't either," Mister said. "Anyway, they're border collies, they're smart, they can learn without a choke chain collar."

I'm good, I can Sit! too, Sadie said to Angus.

I'm not afraid of the collar, he told her.

I'm not either, I just hate it.

No, you're afraid, Angus told her.

Sadie wasn't as sure about that as he was.

They worked on Sit! for days and days, practicing until both of the dogs knew what Sit! meant all of the time, on or off a leash, spoken by Mister or by Missus. They trained and trained, every day, as often as they ate. They had a routine, and at the end Mister or Missus said the words that meant the training was over, *That'll do!*

One evening, after Missus said, "That'll do!" Mister tried something new. He picked up something round and flat and threw it into the air, away from the garden and the house, out into the long grass. Missus and Sadie stood together and watched him. Angus ran up to Mister, to find out what was going on.

"Well, Angus?" Mister asked.

Angus looked at him carefully, trying to figure out how to obey.

"I thought you'd use a ball," Missus said. "I brought a tennis ball."

"Frisbees are better," Mister said. "The book said. Let's try again."

He walked over to pick up the Frisbee, and Angus

went with him. Sadie and Missus stayed where they were.

Mister put the Frisbee down in front of Angus's nose, and Angus smelled a nonsmell and also the smells of Mister's hands and the grass. He sniffed the Frisbee and looked up at Mister. *What's this? What's next? I'm ready!* Mister tossed the Frisbee into the air, back toward Missus, and Angus, without any hesitation—He couldn't wait! Now he'd smelled the Frisbee! He wanted to get it!—he ran after it. He chased after it, and he found it! He picked it up in his mouth, because he'd caught it now. Then he took it back to Mister, so Mister could throw it again and he could find it again, and catch it.

"I knew you'd like this," Mister said.

Fun! This game was much better than Sit! Mister threw the Frisbee, and Angus ran after it. He brought it back and Mister threw it again. Angus ran after it and caught it again. Mister threw and threw, and Angus ran and caught. Twice, he caught the Frisbee before it reached the ground, and Mister laughed. "You're a natural, Angus. It's too bad you're not human, you'd be a terrific outfielder."

Angus didn't know what that was, but he agreed. *Yes! Outfielder! Throw it again!*

There was something about it—When the Frisbee flew out into the air, Angus absolutely *had* to chase it

61

down and bring it back so that Mister could throw it into the air again. Angus ran fast, and faster. He couldn't stop himself and he didn't want to. This was better than anything.

"How about you, Sadie? Don't you want a turn?" Missus said, but Sadie was happy right where she was, next to Missus. She wagged her tail, thumping it softly on the ground.

Missus took a small ball out of her jacket pocket. "Here, try this." She threw the ball away into the grass. It fell down and stopped still. Sadie looked at Missus. "Fetch!" Missus said.

Fetch?

Missus got up and walked over to where the ball lay in the grass. Sadie went with her, to keep her company. Mister had stopped to watch, but Angus didn't want to stop. *I'm here!* he barked, but Mister wasn't paying attention. *Again!* Angus barked.

Missus wanted Sadie to smell the ball, but what did Sadie care how that ball smelled? She walked away, around to the other side of Missus. Then Missus picked up the ball and tossed it back toward the place where she and Sadie had just been sitting. Sadie watched the ball and then she turned to look at Missus. There was something here she didn't understand, and she stared at Missus, waiting for an explanation. But Missus just stared back at her. Then she waved her hand at the ball. "Go get it, girl."

Sadie waited.

I'm right here! I'm ready! Angus stared at Mister, trying to make him understand. But Mister was busy watching Missus and Sadie.

Missus walked back to where the ball was. Sadie walked with her. Missus dropped the ball right in front of Sadie, then kicked it gently with her foot. Sadie watched the ball roll through the grass, until it slowly, slowly stopped. She looked up at Missus.

Mister didn't throw the Frisbee again. Instead, he came over to Missus and Sadie. Angus came right behind him, keeping close to the Frisbee.

"I wonder what's wrong with her," Mister said.

"Didn't the book say that some dogs just don't have any instinct to fetch?" Missus asked him. "Like there are some people who don't like to play cards?"

Me! Me! Angus reminded them. He nudged at the Frisbee in Mister's hand, to remind him of what he was supposed to do.

"I didn't think that would happen with a border collie," Mister said. He kicked the ball with his foot.

All right!

As soon as the ball moved, Angus was moving after it. With one long jump he was on top of it, and had it in his mouth. He brought it back to Mister and dropped it. *Again!*

But when Mister kicked the ball again, he held onto Angus's collar so Angus couldn't go get it. "Go, Sadie!" Mister said.

You do it, Angus said to Sadie.

Do what?

Catch it and bring it back so he can throw it again.

Why?

Because you want to.

But I don't want to.

"I guess you can't predict for sure what will happen with a border collie," Missus said, and she was laughing. "I guess they're as different from one another as everybody else is."

"Looks like it," Mister agreed.

What's wrong with you?

Is something wrong with me? Where?

4
How Angus knows best
and everyone is weird

Although Angus and Sadie slept in the barn, they had their meals on the porch, beside the kitchen door. The water bowls were kept there, too. The other animals were fed once a day, but Angus and Sadie were fed in the morning, at midday, and again in the evening, just like Mister and Missus.

They were fed three times a day, and they had training three times a day. That was their routine. After a couple of weeks, Sit! was simple, but then Mister added something new, Stay! You had to remember to Stay!, even if you wanted to move. Stay! was harder than Sit! They were also learning Come!, which was easy at the end of a Stay!, but not easy when you were digging a hole beside the cow pen or heading off for a drink from the stream.

Everything was easier for Angus than for Sadie, easier to understand at first, and easier to remember after that. Sadie liked the way Angus was so quick and clever, and so did Angus.

You're really smart.

I know.

Let's play!

Missus didn't say "That'll do!"

We could play after.

Maybe. I'll see.

All right.

"Sadie," said Missus, warning her. "Pay attention, you're starting to creep."

Attention! Yes!

One warm, sunny day at the end of May, Angus and Sadie had emptied their food bowls and were waiting for Mister and Missus to finish cleaning their plates so they could have midday training. Angus said to Sadie, *The cows graze all day, eating grass, so really the cows feed themselves, like the barn cats do.* He thought some more. *Mister and Missus feed themselves, too. Because,* he said, as if Sadie had asked him what he meant, *they find their own food. So it's only us and Patches and the chickens that get fed by someone else.*

Are you hungry? I'm not, Sadie answered.

Sometimes, Sadie made no sense at all to Angus.

At that moment, Missus walked out onto the porch, followed by Mister. "We're taking the afternoon off," Missus told them.

Off!

What about my training?

"Only part of the afternoon," Mister said. "And only sort of off. Do you two want to come for a walk?"

Walk, yes!

"We're moving the sheep up to the summer pasture," Missus explained.

Sheep! Remember sheep?

Maybe.

"You'll have to be on leashes," Mister said. "We can't have you upsetting the sheep."

I remember leashes.

"Especially because all four of our lambs have survived," Missus explained, which made no sense to either of the dogs, or to Mister either, but he didn't say so.

"Sheep are weird," Missus said to Mister, as she clipped a leash onto Angus's collar and then another onto Sadie's. "We feed them in their pen behind the barn every day, all winter. We're there to take care of them for the birthings. When they get in trouble, like the sheep Angus found, we help them out. And they still try to run away from us. You'd think they'd trust us."

"You have to remember that we're the ones who tackle them and hold them down when they get sheared," Mister said. "Also, they associate us with shots, and we give them the dips. All those things frighten them."

"I think they have short memories for some things and long memories for other things, and they're always getting it wrong," Missus decided. She held Angus's leash, and Mister held Sadie's. "They really are weird, aren't they?"

Why are we on leashes? Sadie wondered.

Because sheep are weird, Angus explained.

The four of them walked for a long time along the dirt road that led away from the house and barn, back between fields and pastures, up toward the woods. In the hot midday air insects buzzed and hummed, while crows flew around the fields, quarreling.

"This is a perfect day," Missus announced.

"Yes, it is," Mister agreed. "And I keep forgetting to say, your flower garden is looking beautiful."

"The tulips, especially. Don't the reds and yellows cheer you up?"

"So what do you think about this idea: How about turning Angus and Sadie loose in the pasture, before we

68

move the sheep? As an experiment, to see how they react to sheep."

"Aren't they too young?"

"They're almost six months."

"If we're going to turn them loose, why do they have to be on leashes?"

Mister explained, "We won't do that until we're all in the pasture, with the gate closed behind us. Our sheep haven't ever seen dogs before. We don't want them bolting off."

"No, especially not with the lambs."

"But we have to have the dogs back on leashes while I move the flock up to the summer pasture, and you'll have to hold them both then. Can you do that?"

"I'd think so," Missus said. "They're only puppies still, and even if they weren't—I'm a little insulted that you doubt I could do it."

"Oh," said Mister. "You are? But that's not what I meant."

They walked for a long time, and neither Mister nor Missus said anything more.

The spring pasture was a large field, just before the road went into the woods. A rail fence ran around it, but there was no electric wire. There were sheep scattered all around the pasture. Heads down, they ate the sweet spring grass, while the lambs played around them. When

Mister and Missus and the two dogs arrived at the gate, the sheep lifted their heads and stared.

The lambs jumped up, jumped sideways, jumped backward. They ran forward a few steps and jumped some more.

After a brief time, with a little *baa*-ing back and forth as if they were talking it over, the sheep gathered together in a single bunch, the lambs now close beside their ewes. Then, as if an order had been given, the whole flock wheeled around and headed for the far side of the pasture, as far from the gate as they could get. Stopped by the fence, they turned to stare some more at the unwelcome visitors.

The lambs jumped away from the flock, and jumped

back, and jumped sideways.

Mister opened the gate to let the dogs and Missus into the pasture, and then he followed. After he had closed the gate behind them, he said to Missus, "Aren't you curious about what the dogs will do? I am. Sit!" he commanded, and the dogs obeyed. Then Mister and Missus bent down together to let Angus and Sadie off the leashes.

Angus looked at Mister, waiting. Sadie sat beside Angus, waiting with him.

"That'll do!" Mister waved his hand out toward where the sheep were. "Go ahead now."

Let's go! Angus cried, jumping forward. *Let's go see!* He took off, barking in excitement. *Sheep!*

Sadie wasn't sure why it was so exciting, but she barked, too, and ran. Angus crossed the wide pasture and dashed right into the middle of the flock. Sheep scattered in all directions.

With the running and the barking, with the warm day and being let off the leash, with Angus so excited, Sadie became excited, too. But as soon as she got close enough to see the eyes of the sheep, she dropped down to the ground. She didn't think about doing that, she didn't decide to do it, she just did it. She dropped down flat on the ground and stayed there, her eyes fixed on one small group of three sheep.

They watched her back and did not dare to move.

She held them still with her eyes.

Sadie dropped when she saw the sheep, but when Angus saw sheep, he charged them and chased after them. He picked out the one he wanted to Chase! and Catch! and he dashed off at its heels. The sheep ran as fast as it could away from him, and Angus ran as fast as he could after it.

That sheep was a fast runner.

It wheeled around suddenly, and headed off in another direction. Angus wheeled around, right beside its rear legs. Angus was going so fast that he flew right past his sheep, almost running into it, and then he nearly crashed into the bottom rail of the fence.

But that didn't matter because, as he turned, Angus saw two more sheep. They were trying to get away, too, and so he barked at them, and ran.

Sadie stayed down, staring. Her three sheep stayed put, frozen.

She heard some sheep running behind her, their little hooves drumming on the ground, and she heard Angus dashing after them, but she didn't move her eyes from her three. *You're supposed to chase them,* Angus told her as he ran past, but Sadie didn't move one step. She didn't even move an ear.

She moved only when her three sheep took little steps backward, trying to back away from her. When they did that, she moved forward, low on the ground, maintaining her distance.

Angus chased one of his sheep until it stopped, up against the fence, and refused to run anymore. *And stay there,* Angus told it. Then he turned to find a group of four others, which ran and turned and ran and turned, and he ran and turned right behind them. He was as fast as the sheep, and smarter, too. They couldn't outrun him, and they couldn't fool him, either.

After a while, Angus needed a rest, so he lay down in the grass, panting. It didn't take long for him to catch his breath, and while he rested he watched the sheep. They had all stopped running now and were standing around in groups of three and four, grazing again, although they kept their wary eyes on him. The lambs had caught the nervousness of the flock and were now sticking close to their ewes. Angus looked around and saw Mister watching him.

Angus waited for an order, but no order came. He was rested and beginning to look around to choose which sheep to catch next when he noticed a group of three that were not grazing, although they were standing still. They were just standing and staring. They were staring at Sadie, who crouched low on her belly in the grass, staring right back at them.

Angus ran over to join her. *No, no, you make them run away,* he explained. *Like this,* and he ran right at those three sheep.

The sheep hesitated for just a second as if they were making up their minds, and then they broke and ran off together.

Come on, Sadie! Angus dashed after them, running low to the ground, close on the skinny back legs of the slowest.

Sadie got up, and she thought she might follow Angus, but then she saw two sheep grazing together. She dropped down onto the ground again, staring.

The sheep didn't notice her, so she crept up closer, never standing up, never moving her eyes from them. As soon as they did notice her, she stopped.

They stopped, too—stopped dead in their tracks with grass hanging out of their mouths.

Nobody moved. Sadie settled in to be sure those two sheep didn't even think about moving. She held them with her eyes. She was not distracted by Angus running around, chasing sheep back and forth behind her, beside her, in front of her, and as long as she was not distracted, her two sheep stayed put.

Finally, when Angus had stopped to rest again and the flock—except for Sadie's two—were quietly grazing again, Mister called, "Angus, Come!"

By then Angus was ready to sit by Mister.

"Sadie, Come!" Missus called. After not hearing her, then pretending not to hear her, Sadie finally, reluctantly, obeyed. She knew those sheep would sneak away as soon as she took her eyes off them. She tried to turn around every few steps, to keep them where they should be, but that didn't work, so she gave up and ran over to sit by Missus. The leashes were clipped on again.

"They're border collies all right," Mister said. "Angus is a natural herder. Did you see him go after them?"

"Sadie kept hers in place," Missus said.

"That's not herding," Mister said.

"Well, I think you did just fine, Sadie," Missus said. "Did you enjoy it?" To Angus she said, "I know *you* had a good time. Anyone could see that." She took both leashes in her hand.

Missus and the dogs went out through the gate and didn't close it behind them. They walked a little way along the dirt road, and then waited. In the pasture, Mister waved his arms and called out loud sounds— "Hunh! Hohn! Coo-eee!"—which made the sheep gather all together into a flock—except for the lambs, who, once the dogs had gone, had returned to jumping up and down wherever they wanted. When he had the flock gathered, Mister flapped his arms and shouted some more. "Hey! Hey, hoo-eee! Sheep!" He waved and shouted from behind the flock, and the sheep, as if they had been trained to do this, trotted together, the lambs next to their ewes, across the pasture and out the gate.

They walked for a long time, Missus and the dogs in the lead and then the flock of sheep—the lambs quiet now, busy just keeping up—and then Mister at the rear. He flapped his arms and shouted whenever any of the sheep started to break loose from the flock. On his leash, Angus knew that he wasn't supposed to try to catch the sheep now. In fact, he wasn't all that eager to do any more running and chasing, not right then. He was sort of tired, and glad that Missus held onto the leash while they walked along, leading the sheep and Mister up the dirt road.

The road went uphill into the woods, and they walked among tall leafy trees, and tall needly trees, too, some of which had a sharp, thick smell of their own, different from any other. They walked for a long time, until Angus and Sadie were ready for a drink of water, and then they emerged from the trees onto a grassy hillside, where large boulders were rising up through the ground. A stream rushed down across this hill, and Missus took Angus and Sadie over to drink out of it. The sheep seemed to remember this place because they immediately scattered in small groups and began to graze, their heads close to the grass, *baa*-ing occasionally at one another. Their short tails twitched, and the lambs started jumping again. There was no fence, but the sheep didn't try to run away.

Sheep are weird, Angus remarked to Sadie.

You mean, the way they forget right away about being frightened? Sadie asked. Because she was on the leash, she didn't have to worry about keeping her eyes on some sheep, to stop them from running off.

No, I mean the way they're so easy to frighten. Even more than you, Angus said.

I'm only frightened sometimes. And only by some things.

All the time, Angus corrected her. *Anything. But not as much as sheep, and that's pretty good.*

Sadie was content to be pretty good.

For a while, they all stood together in the sunlight, watching the sheep. Then Mister and Missus sat down on one of the big boulders, with Angus and Sadie lying in front of them.

"What a day," Missus said. "It's perfect, absolutely perfect, a perfect May day."

"See the way they keep looking over, to check up on us?"

"The dogs? The dogs are asleep."

"No, the sheep. The dogs make them nervous, and so do we. But they're not bolting."

"Well, it's not as if they were wild animals. A wild animal—a deer, for example—would have run off long since, back into the woods."

"But they're not tame, either, not like the cows. But—see? They only wander off a certain distance, and then they stop as if there was a fence up here, too, to keep them in, instead of only woods and the steep hill. Maybe it's because they've got plenty to eat right here?"

"I've never understood sheep," Missus said. "But they give wool. Really, they're as much like a garden as like an animal, if you think about it. We harvest them, don't we? The only difference is, we harvest them in spring, not fall."

Mister turned to stare at Missus. "You're pretty weird yourself," he told her.

Then it was summer. In summer, the days were hotter, mostly, and sunny, although sometimes they were gray and rainy. On the farm, summer was a lazy time, with only weeding and watering to be done, and the cows and chickens to be taken care of, of course, and the sheep to be checked up on every now and then, and the training routine to continue. In summer, the leaves on the trees were so thick that they rustled in the slightest breeze and rain fell through them with pitter-pattering sounds. The best thing about summer was the way it went on and on, day after slow day.

Starting in July, Angus and Sadie were fed just twice a day, in the morning and in the evening, and they were trained three times, after breakfast, at midday, and after supper. They were learning to Heel!, with the leash keeping them close to Mister or Missus's left side. When they were heeling, they had to turn whenever Mister or Missus turned, and stop, sitting when they stopped. It took a lot of close attention to Heel! Angus was better at heeling because he was better at paying close attention.

When the summer evenings stretched out warm and golden, Mister and Missus liked to go outside after supper. First, they had training, and then, while Missus sat with Sadie to watch, Mister threw the Frisbee for Angus to catch, and they talked.

"I bet Angus ends up a better work dog than my brother's Lucy," Mister said. "Don't you think he will?"

"I have no idea," answered Missus. "But you should praise Sadie, too. She might not be as good as Angus, but she's still good."

"Sadie doesn't mind," Mister said. "Do you, girl?"

Mind what?

"I hope not," Missus said.

Again! Throw again!

During summer the mice and rats found plenty of food outside, so Fox and Snake sometimes came out from the barn in the evening. They watched the goings-on and commented. Of course, they commented loudly enough for Angus to hear and care. Sadie could hear, too, but she didn't care.

Lookit that, Snake called over to Fox. *Look what he's doing now.*

That is one weird dog, Fox called back to Snake. *It's not as if he can eat it.*

Snake explained, *You catch it while it's flying. I wouldn't mind trying.*

But don't you see? They have to throw it for you to catch. If you want them to do that, you might as well be a dog.

Who are you calling a dog? Snake demanded.

When Angus answered that—*I'm a dog and I'm proud of it. Who'd want to be a cat?*—they ignored him, as if they hadn't even heard him. Then he saw the Frisbee move through the air again, and all he could think about was catching it, deciding if he would jump up—high!—and catch it out of the air, or if he would run—fast!—so he'd be waiting for it as it descended. While Angus was chasing and catching the Frisbee, he didn't hear anyone, not the cats' snide comments, not Mister's praise or Missus's applause, not even Sadie's excited barking. After, when he was running to bring the Frisbee back to Mister, he did hear the applause and the excitement, and he liked that just as much as he really did not like the cats' insults.

Sadie had a special summer job, which was to keep Missus company at the farm stand at the end of the driveway. In the mornings, Mister helped Missus load the back of the pickup with eggs fresh from the chickens and whatever was ripe from the garden. They drove down to a little three-sided building close to the mailbox. The building held two long tables, upon which Missus set out peas, bags of lettuces, green and red peppers, baskets of beans, spinach—whatever she had ready to sell. Sometimes, Missus had made butter, which she kept in a special cooler so it wouldn't melt. All morning, Missus sat in a chair in the shade and read a book or sewed on her quilt, and waited for cars to stop while Sadie, on a leash, napped beside her.

Sometimes the people from the cars paid attention to

Sadie. "Hello, dog. What do you have today by way of lettuce?" Sadie would wag her tail and get patted on the head or ears. If there was a child with the customer, the child would run right over to Sadie. Then Sadie would run to hide behind Missus's legs, because who knew what a child might do? "She doesn't like children," Missus would explain.

"That's pretty weird, for a dog," the customer would say. "She won't bite, will she? Do you have any of your butter today?"

Am I weird? Sadie asked Angus.

Sort of. But I'm not—no matter what those cats say.

Sometimes, when Mister and Angus came home in the evening after a day of fixing fences or clearing fallen trees or working with the tractor in the fields, and after Mister milked the cows, there would be company for supper. Mister and Missus, Sadie and Angus would all go out to the porch, to welcome the guests.

Some guests came with a dog of their own. The guests would sit and talk, and then have supper and talk some more. They might all take a walk together, or throw Frisbees for the dogs to catch, or practice Sit! and Heel! The guests never brought cats, or children, although sometimes they talked about children and having babies. At the end, when it was dark, the guests would drive away in their car, as Mister and Missus, Sadie and Angus stood on the porch watching.

One evening, it wasn't a guest who arrived. Angus and Mister were just coming in from the barn when a car, almost as big as Mister's pickup, drove up. A strange man climbed down from it and waited for them.

Angus didn't like the smell of him, and Mister didn't either, Angus could tell, so he barked twice in warning. *Hey, you. You!*

Sadie and Missus came out of the house to see from the porch what was going on.

You better get away! Angus barked and Sadie echoed him, *Get away!*

"Sadie, Sit!" Missus said, and Sadie obeyed. "Sit! Angus," said Mister, and Angus obeyed, but he kept his eye on the stranger.

"Are these working dogs?" the stranger asked.

"This is a farm," Mister told him. "We all work here."

"I meant trialing. But I know what you mean, and I won't waste your time. I know how busy you farmers are this time of year. See, I just bought a condo up on the mountain—we're great skiers, the whole family—and I'd like to do some hunting here in the fall. Deer," he said.

"I've got cows," Mister said, "and sheep. And the dogs, too. Our land is posted, no hunting."

"I saw that. But the property owner can give permission for someone to hunt on his land, can't he?"

"Well, yes," Mister said. "But I don't want to do that."

"I should have said, I'd pay you for it."

"I don't think so," Mister said.

"I should have said, I'd pay a lot."

"It's not that I'm hurrying you off," Mister said, "but my wife has dinner on the table."

"Here's my card," the stranger said, and passed a little piece of white paper to Mister, who looked at it, and then put it into his pocket. "Call me when you've had a chance to think things over." He climbed back up into his big car and backed it around, then drove away.

Mister and Missus, Angus and Sadie all watched the big car go down the driveway, raising dust behind it. "Good barking, Angus," Mister said.

I had good barking.

And I helped.

Mister took the piece of paper out of his pocket, and ripped it in half.

"You really took against him," Missus said.

"He was throwing his money around," Mister explained. "And he drives an SUV."

That started Missus laughing. "You really are weird, you know that?"

Mister laughed, too. "No, I'm not. I'm normal. He's the one who's weird."

I don't understand weird, Sadie said.

It's what's not normal, Angus explained. *It's what's different from me.*

5

How Missus, Angus, and Sadie harvest blueberries, while Mister harvests hay and Fox harvests a rat

After summer had been going on for quite a while, Mister said it was time to harvest the hay and alfalfa, to use for winter feed and to sell at the farmer's cooperative. Missus said it was time to gather blueberries for jam. The machines that came to cut and bale the hay were large, and loud, and dangerous, and Mister had to give all of his attention to that job. So Missus took both Sadie and Angus with her to the blueberry fields, which were on high land in the hills beyond the woods. To get there, Missus needed the tractor, with a cart attached behind it.

"I like driving the tractor on the old logging trails,"

Missus said. "It's an adventure, the way it bounces and lurches. It's a test of my strength."

"Stick to the roads," Mister warned her. "I don't want to have to come pull you out of some ditch."

"There are no roads," she laughed, "so there can't be ditches. But I'll stick to the ruts."

"The dogs should ride in the cart," Mister decided. "They'll distract you if they're in the cab."

Once Missus was seated up in the tractor cab, and the motor was rumbling, Angus jumped up into the cart. Sadie didn't want to. *Come on,* Angus urged her. *Everybody's waiting for you.*

You said I should stay away from the tractor.

But this is a cart. Besides, I'm here so you don't have to be afraid.

I'm not afraid. I don't think I am. Am I?

Just jump!

Sadie jumped in, and Missus started off. The dogs stood on their hind legs, with their front paws on the side of the cart, so they could watch everything.

The bright air was hot and soaked in sunlight. As the tractor pulled the cart up the dirt road, the dogs were knocked gently around and bounced softly up and down. Every time they fell down, they climbed back up on the wooden sides, waiting to be knocked and bounced again. The picnic basket bounced with them, and so did the two jugs full of water, a bucket for gathering, and empty cartons to hold the blueberries.

Fun! Angus said when he bounced, but Sadie wasn't sure she agreed. It didn't feel like fun to her. It felt like horrible loud noises, and horrible falling over, and horrible tractor smells, and she wanted it to stop. She wanted not to be in the cart. She wanted to be back in the quiet house with Patches. *Oouff!* said Sadie. *Ouch!*

The tractor went more slowly once it entered the cool, shady woods. In the cart, however, the two dogs and the picnic basket and the bucket and the empty cartons bounced even higher than before. Insects buzzed around them, but the noise of the tractor warned birds and animals away. The tractor lurched through the woods for a long time, climbing until it came out onto a rocky hillside.

Missus drove up to the top of the hill and stopped. She turned off the motor.

For a minute, in that sudden silence, Sadie and Angus couldn't hear anything. Everybody stayed still for that minute, Missus on the tractor seat with her hands in her lap, listening, Angus staring at Missus, waiting, and Sadie hearing her own heartbeat slow down again. Then Sadie started to hear everything.

She heard the big machines at work harvesting the fields, so far away they were just a soft humming in the distance, as friendly as the wind. She heard birds chirping songs and insects buzzing. She heard how the breeze rustled through the grass before it rattled its way through the bushes. And stretching out behind every other sound, Sadie could hear the deep silence of the boulders that pushed up through the ground, up into the air.

Then she heard Missus speak softly. "All right," Missus said, and she climbed down from the tractor seat. "Angus, Come!" she said. "Sadie, Come!"

The two dogs clambered over the side of the cart, leaping down onto the ground. Sadie was so glad to be back on the ground she ran in two big circles, and then two more. Angus was not so silly. He poked all around, checking things out, sniffing for smells that could warn of trouble or danger. Missus reached into the cart for the bucket. "All right," she said again. "You two have a good time. I've got work to do," and she walked away across the hillside, then crouched down on her heels. Her fingers got to work, pulling the blueberries off their stems and dropping them into the bucket.

I have work to do, too, Angus said, and headed back down toward the woods.

I don't, said Sadie, and she was not a bit sorry about that.

Sadie looked around her, and sniffed the air. It smelled of grass and dirt, trees and undergrowth in the

woods, and a delicate, sharp, sweet something. She raised
her nose and smelled old, faded sheep smells, wool and
manure, and then she noticed things moving through
the air just over the ground, little things with wings, bigger than insects, much bigger than flies and wasps and
hornets and bees, but much, much smaller than birds.
She noticed all the different shapes of rocks, some tall
and huge, some low and flat. She noticed the clear sky.
She noticed everything.

Angus had disappeared into the woods, so Sadie went
to join Missus. Missus reached down into the grass to
pick berries, and then dropped them into her bucket.

When the basket was full, she went back to the tractor and gently poured the berries into one of the cartons. She gave one little round berry to Sadie, who liked being fed a treat even though she didn't particularly care for the treat itself. But the blueberry tasted like that delicate, sharp, sweet smell, so now she knew what it was. She also knew she didn't want any more, so she didn't follow Missus back to the field. Instead, Sadie thought maybe she should go into the woods. That was what Angus had done and Angus did things right.

Off in the woods, Angus barked. Sadie wondered what he was chasing after, or chasing off, and decided she'd rather explore everything in the field, in the scrub grasses, and all around the rocks. A crow sat on one of the rocks and Sadie ran up to it, *Bark! Bark!* When the crow flew off—*Caw! Caw!*—she ran barking after it, just for fun. You couldn't catch birds, not if you were a dog. She knew that. If you were a cat, if you were Fox or Snake, you sometimes did, although you could never catch a crow. But Sadie wasn't a cat. It was easy for birds to fly away from dogs, but Sadie still liked to run as fast as she could after the bird, as if she *might* catch it.

The sun rose higher in the sky, and the day grew hotter. When Missus brought the bucket back to the tractor cart again, she called both dogs. "Angus, Come!" she called loudly, toward the woods. "Sadie, Come!" she called more quietly, because she could see Sadie with her nose stuck deep into the long grass. "You need water and so do I," Missus told the dogs. She set down two bowls that she filled with water from a jug, and then she lifted the jug to her mouth and drank, too.

I needed water, Sadie said, *and Missus knew it.*

There were deer in the woods, Angus reported, and then lapped away at his bowl, five or six times. *Big ones and little ones. I almost caught a raccoon.* He lapped some more. *I saw a fox, too, with cubs.* Before Sadie had time to say anything, he told her, *I didn't see any bears, but I smelled one. I think that's what it was.*

What do bears smell like? Sadie wondered.

You don't want to know, Angus told her. He didn't like to think of what might happen to Sadie if she ran into a bear. Or a raccoon, for that matter. *Stay away from raccoons, too,* he warned Sadie. *You better stay out of the woods.*

All right.

Missus finished her water and the dogs finished theirs, so she went back to her berry gathering. The dogs sat in the shade of the tractor, and Angus stretched out on the cool grass to sleep.

Sadie didn't want to sleep. She heard Missus in the bushes, talking softly, maybe talking to the blueberries as she dropped them into her bucket. She heard Angus snuffling in his sleep, dreaming. She heard the breeze ruffling along the top of the grass. She saw some more of the little flying things, hovering there, in the breeze just above the grass.

They didn't fly like insects, busily hurrying some-place. They didn't fly the way birds flew, soaring up, sweeping down, gliding across. Instead, they fluttered from anywhere to somewhere else, as if they didn't care where they were or where they were going. Sadie went over to see them close up. They didn't fly away from her like birds and insects did, or circle around her like the cats did. They just hovered, float-ing up, floating down.

When Sadie crept even closer, they still didn't pay any attention to her. So she jumped right into the middle of them and ran with them through the grass. Her feet ran on the grassy ground, and their wings fluttered in the air.

Sadie turned around to follow another bunch, run-ning to catch up with them, jumping through the grass. She couldn't tell one from the other, and they didn't smell at all as she moved among them, going first after one, then another, then another and another. It felt wonderful, twisting and running, jumping and turning in the sunny air. She wondered if the little flying things were afraid of her, but she didn't think so. She wondered if they were playing with her, but she didn't think so. She wondered if they even noticed she was there, or if they knew she wouldn't hurt them.

Missus told Mister about it that evening, after they had rumbled and bumped their way back home late in the afternoon, and the blueberries had been washed and put away in the icebox for the next day's jam making. Mister was showered clean after his day in the hayfields, and the animals lay resting, the dogs on the floor, Patches on the windowsill behind the sink. Missus and Mister were eating supper. Missus said, "It was like she was dancing. Dancing with moths."

"She was trying to catch them," Mister decided.

No I wasn't.

"No she wasn't," Missus said. "Most of the time, her mouth wasn't even open."

"Then what?" Mister asked. "If she won't chase a Frisbee or a ball, you have to admit she has no fetching instinct. So what do you think she was doing with the moths?"

"I told you. Dancing. You were having a good time, weren't you, Sadie?"

Yes!

"Dogs don't dance," Mister pointed out. "And not with moths, and they don't chase insects either. I don't get it, Sadie. What were you up to?"

Dancing! I was dancing! They were dancing! Were they moths?

I don't get it either, Angus said, but Patches spoke up from his safe place above the sink and across the room from Angus. *I do.*

Harvesting the hayfields took the men two days, but picking blueberries took only one, so on the second day Angus and Sadie stayed inside with Missus in the hot kitchen to get away from the noise.

Missus made jam on the stove and poured it into jars. She then sealed the jars with paraffin. Everything she did made it even hotter in the kitchen, so hot that even Patches went outside. He went no farther than the porch, but still, for him, the porch was pretty far out. However, even though it was much cooler there, the horrible noise of the machine—cutting and baling, clanking, roaring, and occasionally screeching—drove Patches back inside. He went upstairs and found a closet to sleep in for the rest of the day.

Sadie went up with Patches for a while, although Sadie went under the bed, not into the closet. She had a little nap, and then she returned to the kitchen to help Missus and keep her company. Then she went upstairs again, and then she came downstairs again, and that was how she spent the day.

When he couldn't take the kitchen heat another minute, Angus went out onto the porch. When he couldn't take the noise another minute, he went down to the barn. The barn was shady and not as hot as the yard or the kitchen. The barn was noisy, but not as noisy as the porch. When he entered through the wide doorway, coming into the shade from bright sunlight, he couldn't see anything at first. He only heard Fox. Fox said, *Whatsa matter? Nobody got any use for you?*

Not right now. There was a sour, heavy smell in the air. Fox was over behind buckets and shovels and rakes and hoes. There was a crunching sound, smushing sounds, eating sounds. Angus could see Fox now, holding something between her paws.

Got me a rat, Fox said. *Have some.*

Now that he could see it, Angus said, *That's disgusting.*

My job is to catch them.

And eat them, too? Angus's meals were good brown, crunchy bits, topped with a spoonful of special soft food from a can, and eaten out of a bright metal bowl. How could Fox eat that thing?

Eating's part of the job.

I'd rather have my job.

You mean your job as Mister's slave?

What do you mean, slave?

A slave does what he's told, like Sadie's your slave.

I am not, Angus said. *So what if I am? So are you.*

Oh yeah? Nobody tells me what to do or when to do it. I catch my own food.

Crunch, smush, she went on eating while Angus thought about that.

I could catch my own. I just don't want to.

Ha. Ha-ha. The way you let them tell you what to eat and what to do?

You aren't even allowed in the house.

As if I wanted to.

Angus walked away. You could never win an argument with a cat, even if you were right. He decided he'd go find Sadie and make her come with him to watch the big harvesting machine. It wasn't good for her to be so afraid of everything.

6

How Sadie meets a skunk, dances with light, and locates two sheep

As summer came to an end, the days grew shorter and cooler. Then it was September. Mister used his tractor to bring in the baled hay, stacking it in the barn loft, and Missus no longer sold eggs and vegetables at the farm stand. Instead, in the morning she picked tomatoes in the garden, so that in the afternoon she could skin them and chop them and get them into the freezer for winter. Now that evening came earlier, Mister and Missus liked to sit together on the porch steps after dinner, to talk and listen and watch as the forests and hills, stream, farm, and fields faded away into darkness. But, on one of those evenings, just as they were finishing their supper, Missus said, "It's about time to board up the farm stand."

"Let's do it right now," Mister decided. "There's still enough light. We'll take the pickup to carry back the tables and baskets, and I'll bring my toolbox so I can winterize the shed. Ready?"

Angus and Sadie—who always ate more quickly than the humans, and were resting by the kitchen stove—knew what "ready" meant. Both dogs jumped up and went to the door. They stood there, ready.

"Look at those two," Missus said, and she laughed.

"I guess they can come with us," Mister decided. "Let's go, Angus, Sadie." He held the kitchen door open.

The dogs ran out, jumped down the steps, and dashed to the truck, which was parked in front of the barn. When Mister caught up with them, he lowered the transom, and they jumped up onto the bed. He closed the transom behind them.

They bounced along down the dirt driveway to the farm stand. Sadie wanted to tell Angus about the ditches, and everything she'd found there over the summer, but Angus was thinking about something else. *Mister is the boss of everyone. He's the one who decides everything. Have you noticed?*

No.

He's the boss, so I'm supposed to do what he says. And so should you.

I try.

Try harder.

All right. But will you come into the ditch? Sometimes, I can smell something. Maybe it's a squirrel, or maybe a rac-coon.

Or a skunk.

What's a skunk?

Something you don't want to meet up with. Mister said.

All right, I won't.

Or maybe a porcupine.

What's that?

Something else you never want to meet. Don't worry, Sadie. Maybe it's a fox. I'd recognize that smell.

If it's a fox smell in the ditch, you can tell me and then I'll know it, too.

When the truck stopped at the farm stand, Mister didn't come around to let them jump out. He told them, "Angus, Stay! Sadie, Stay!" then said to Missus, "Let's get to work. You load up the rear while I check out the building."

Angus pointed this out to Sadie. *See what I mean about Mister deciding? Everybody does what Mister tells them to.*

I want to go to the ditch, Sadie said.

Mister said Stay! You have to.

They waited, standing with their front paws on the edge of the pickup bed, watching Missus stack baskets into piles and getting out of the way when she dumped the piles into the back of the truck, watching Mister walk all around the inside of the stand and then all around the outside. Sometimes he hammered at a board. After Missus carried baskets out to the pickup, she dragged out the two long pieces of wood that made the tops of the tables, and put them in, too. The back of the truck was getting crowded, but the dogs stayed put, as they had been told.

"Good dogs," Missus said.

"Good dogs," Mister said. "Let me help with the saw-horses."

It was dark by the time they jounced back along the driveway to stop in front of the big barn door. "You take the tables into the barn," Mister said, as he lowered the transom at the back of the truck.

"The baskets go on the porch," Missus said. "For storing potatoes and carrots in the cellar."

"That'll do! Angus," Mister said to the dogs. "That'll do! Sadie." Angus and Sadie jumped down out of the truck, and that's when trouble began.

Because Sadie saw something. She saw something moving. A shadow darker than the dark air moved in the garden.

Look!

She barked two short sharp barks. At the same time, she ran.

What she had seen seemed like a cat, but it didn't run like a cat. What she had seen was black and bright white, and it was humping along through the shadows.

Mister called out in a big, loud voice. "Angus, Sit! Stay! Sadie, Sit!"

"Oh no," Missus said, as Sadie passed her and kept on running. Missus was on her way to the porch, where the not-a-cat was also headed. "No, Sadie. Leave it—"

"Sadie, Sit!" roared Mister.

Sadie couldn't stop, and she didn't want to. She was going to chase this animal away even if Angus wasn't going to show her how and help her. The animal was running away from her, and she was chasing it away.

Missus put the baskets down on the ground and hurried back to the truck, and Mister, and Angus. "Good dog, Angus. Good sitting, good staying," she said.

Sadie went right after that strange animal. *Get out! Get away from the house! Go away! Or I'll—*

The animal stopped and turned to look at her.

Sadie stopped, too. She was much bigger than it was. *Out! Get out!*

The animal stamped its front foot. Stamp, stamp, stamp.

Sadie wasn't afraid of any stamping. She started

toward it, and growled. *Or you'll be sorry.*

The animal stopped stamping and turned around. Sadie took a couple of quick steps forward, ready to run after it some more and finish chasing it away. It raised its tail up into the air and—

Terrible! Help! Stop! Angus!

Sadie turned and ran, howling and howling. Her eyes burned! She couldn't see!

Help! It hurts!

And then she ran as fast as she could to get away from the smell. That smell was horrible. She didn't like to breathe it in, and she couldn't get away from it. It was following her—no, it wasn't following her—it *was* her.

The horrible nasty scary smell was all over her!

Sadie ran up to Missus, who was hiding behind Mister, who was hiding behind the truck.

Don't come near me, Angus warned her.

"It was a skunk," Missus said.

"It had to happen sooner or later," Mister said. "Maybe this will teach her to obey."

I told you, Angus said.

Help! cried Sadie, and she didn't care who helped her as long as she could stop feeling so horrible.

"All right, all right. Come! Sadie," Mister said.

Sadie came.

"Sit!" Mister said, when she was still a distance away from him.

Sadie sat.

"Good dog, now, Stay!" Mister said. "We'll get some— do we have any lemons? Any tomato juice? You go up and see what we have, and I'll get the tub out, and the hose. Smart dog, Angus, keep your distance from her."

How can I help you if you don't obey? Angus explained.

I will now, Sadie said, and she meant it. She sat there, shaking. This was the worst thing that had ever happened to her.

They covered her with sharp-smelling tomato juice, and they rubbed her with canned tomatoes, too, and then they washed her with soap and hosed her down.

But she could still smell her own terrible smell. Angus wouldn't sleep in the stall with her that night, and all the next day, Missus wouldn't let her into the house.

"You stink, Sadie," they all said.

She did stink, she knew it, and she was sorry. But she didn't want them telling her that all the time, all day, even if it was true. That night, however, Angus returned to their stall to sleep on the blanket with her, so Sadie could begin to stop remembering.

After the skunk, the days kept on getting shorter and the air colder until one day Missus dug potatoes and carrots out of the garden and carried them down into the cellar in big bushel baskets. Later, in the middle of the night, Angus heard something.

Wake up! he said to Sadie. *We have work to do.*

Where? What? Angus?

There's something in the garden. Follow me!

What if it's a skunk?

Don't worry, I'm going first. I'll tell you if it is.

Angus ran out of the barn, barking. Sadie, also barking, followed, but she kept back behind Angus, in case it might turn out to be a skunk. She could see something shambling along, moving away, around the back of the barn. Angus didn't chase it. He stayed in the garden, barking. Then, *Gone. Only a raccoon,* he said.

The dogs returned to their stall, but it wasn't long before Angus woke Sadie up again. *They're back! Stay behind me! Don't worry, they're afraid when we bark.* He ran out of the barn, barking and barking and barking. Sadie followed at a distance, and she barked, too. This time Mister and Missus came running outside, slamming the kitchen door and thumping their feet on the steps.

"What is it?" Missus asked.

Mister said, "Something in the garden. Raccoons? I can't see, and I can't hear a thing with all this noise the dogs are making."

"I'll get the flashlight," Missus said.

Now the dogs could see two—no, four—raccoons at the back of the garden. The four raccoons didn't run away the way the solitary raccoon had. All four turned to look at Angus, and all four showed their sharp teeth, snarling.

Angus wasn't afraid. He was bigger than any two of them put together. He barked and charged.

Sadie *was* afraid. She remembered the skunk, and besides, she didn't like the gleaming white look of those teeth. She stood where she was and barked.

Finally, when Angus was almost close enough to grab a leg in his teeth, the raccoons turned and shambled away, the way raccoons move when they move fast. *That's right! And don't even think about coming back!* Angus told them.

By now, Mister and Missus had come out to the garden. On the ground right in front of them was something—something bright, like daylight, like sunlight, but small like a rock, and flat like a puddle, and it slid over the ground like a snake.

Sadie forgot about raccoons. She was busy watching the light.

She watched it flow over the grass in front of Mister and Missus, and then she watched it bump up and down over the dirt in the garden. It tried to climb up the tomato stalks and it tried to hide in the leaves around the pumpkin vines. It moved all over everything, like a moth, and then it moved back and forth and in circles on the ground near Mister and Missus.

Of course Sadie followed it. She put her nose out at it, put her nose right into it, to smell what it was, but it smelled of the grass and the dirt, the tomato stalks and the pumpkin leaves. It had no smell of its own. She tried to get close to it, but it slipped away. So she chased it, moving right along with it, sometimes stepping on it, sometimes backing away, turning and turning. It moved around as if it was trying to get away, but also as if it might want to chase her back. It was just like one of the moths from the summer, only much bigger and not flying in the air.

Sadie didn't try to catch it, any more than she had tried to catch the moth. What would be the point of catching it? The point was being right there with it, right behind, right beside, right ahead of. It was a game of With, not Catch.

"What is she doing?" Mister asked. Missus was laughing, now, and he started laughing, too. "I mean, it's only a flashlight. What does she *think* it is?"

"It's what I told you this summer, she's dancing. Look at her."

The bright thing started moving faster, in a circle. Sadie moved faster, too, keeping up. It moved back and forth, then around, and Sadie moved back and forth and turned around, too. She jumped up and landed, jumped and turned and landed.

Mister and Missus were laughing and laughing.

"Dancing it is," Mister said. "You're something else, Sadie."

Yes!

"What about you, Angus?" Mister asked. "Don't you want to dance? No, you wouldn't. You know that dogs don't dance."

Yes. I know. But it was exciting to watch Sadie, and Angus barked a couple of times from the excitement of Sadie dancing and Mister and Missus laughing.

After a while Missus said, "Let's get back to bed," and the puddle of light went away, leaving them all in sudden darkness.

"Good work keeping those raccoons out, Angus,"

Mister said. "Good work dancing, Sadie."

Mister and Missus returned to the house, and Angus and Sadie returned to their stall. They curled up close to each other for warmth, and Angus said, *I can learn everything. Teach me how to dance.*

You just—I just—do it. I don't know how to teach something.

That's right, Angus said. *You don't. Oh well. It's lucky I do, so I can teach you all the things I know.*

It was cold the next morning. A thin layer of ice lay on top of the dogs' water bowl, but sunlight soon warmed the air. After morning training and chores, Mister drove the tractor out of the barn, and then stopped it and climbed down while it was still running. He called Angus. "What do you say we check on the sheep?"

Angus came to sit in front of Mister. He watched Mister's face and waited to find out what Mister wanted him to do.

"You, too, dancing dog," Mister said. "Sadie, Come!"

Sadie came. She sat beside Angus, and they both watched Mister's face. Sadie's tail wagged back and forth across the ground.

"Get in, Angus. You, too, Sadie." Mister held the door open. Angus jumped up into the cab, but Sadie didn't move.

Come on, said Angus. *Don't keep Mister waiting.*

"Sadie, Come!" Mister said.

But—but it's the tractor.

Mister's voice warned. "Sadie? Come!"

Angus said, *When I'm here it's safe.*

Mister's voice got deep. "Sadie! Come!"

Sadie had to obey, and she did. She came slowly, slowly, close to the tractor, climbed slowly up and found herself in the cab. The tractor smelled terrible inside. Then Mister climbed in, too, and shut the door.

Sadie's ears ached with the grinding roar of the motor. Her bones rattled. Even standing still that tractor shook. And then it started moving.

Sadie crowded up beside Angus. She was shaking, and the tractor was shaking, too.

The tractor not only shook, but also bounced as it went along the dirt road, traveling alongside the fields on its way up to the pastures. Sadie bounced into Angus, and he bounced back into her, and they both bounced into Mister. Then Sadie stopped noticing the horrible noises and the horrible smells. Instead, she noticed the bouncing.

Bounce! Bounce!

It's not a game, Sadie. We have work to do.

Look out! Here I bounce!

When the tractor halted, they were in a grassy pasture with big boulders. Mister climbed down. Angus and

Sadie jumped down after him. "Angus, Sit! Stay!" said Mister. Angus sat.

"Sadie, Sit!" Mister said, but Sadie smelled rocks and sheep and soil, woods and grass and sunshine. The air came so cold and fresh into her mouth, she wanted to run in big circles. So she did. She ran in one big circle, and then another, and had started on a third when she saw the sheep. And stopped dead. She got her sights on one sheep, eyeing it. That sheep knew better than to try to get away from her.

Then Mister called her. "Sadie, Come!"

Without hesitation, Sadie rose and went to him.

"Good dog. Now Angus, Heel! Sadie, Come!"

Stay with me. Do what I do. Pay attention.

The three of them approached the flock of sheep, Mister leading, Angus just behind Mister's left foot and sticking close. Sadie stayed a little way behind Angus. As they got closer, the sheep looked up, but they didn't see anything to worry about so they went right back to grazing on the rich fall grass. Coming close to the sheep, Sadie had to stop. She crouched low and flat again, eyeing two of them, but Mister said, "Sadie, Come!" and she got up, reluctantly, to obey.

Sheep were scattered all over the pasture, in groups. Sadie even saw a pair off behind a big rock, their heads close to the ground.

Mister went in the other direction with Angus at his heels and Sadie behind them. "That's eight," Mister said, "ten, eleven . . ."

What is he doing?

Checking on the sheep. What he said.

What are we doing?

I'm heeling.

Sadie followed along, with the air sweet in her mouth and the soft, confused voices of the sheep in her ears.

"Sixteen," Mister said, "seventeen, eighteen," as he approached another group of sheep. They backed away from him. "Sadie," he said, in a warning voice, "Come!" How did he know that she was about to drop down and get an eye on those sheep?

Then Mister was finished, and he repeated, "Angus, Heel!" when he turned to go back to the tractor. "Sadie, Come!"

He didn't check those other ones. Why didn't he check them? Sadie asked.

What other ones? Where are you going?

They're over behind—

Wait. I have to heel first. Follow me, Sadie.

Sadie followed. After Angus had heeled obediently all the way back to the tractor, he barked.

"What is it?" Mister asked.

Angus turned toward the rocks. *This way?*

That's right, I saw—

Angus barked twice, sharply, and ran to the rocks.

When Angus—followed by Sadie, who was followed by Mister—came around the boulder and saw them, the two sheep raised their heads to see what was happening. Sadie dropped down and eyed them, so they wouldn't run away.

"Angus, Sit!" Mister said. "That's nineteen and twenty. Good for you, Angus. Clever dog. That's all of them."

Clever me, too, Sadie said.

You didn't bark, Angus explained

At dinner time, Mister told Missus about it. "I'd have wasted all morning looking for those other two if he hadn't found them for me. He's a natural, I keep telling you."

"Yes, you do," Missus agreed.

"I have to look up the requirements, but I'd like to try him in an obedience class competition. Maybe in the spring? If we work hard all winter."

"What about Sadie?" Missus asked.

"She's going to take a lot longer to get well-trained. But she has her own special talent, don't you? Dancing Dog, that's you, Sadie. The only dancing dog in the world, maybe. But you, Angus, have some work ahead of you. How do you feel about hard work?"

Angus was half asleep so he just wagged his tail. Thump, thump, his tail slapped against the floor.

I can work hard, Sadie said. *I think I can. Do you think I can? Because I found the sheep, too, didn't I?*

It's not the same if you don't bark, Angus explained patiently.

7
How it's fall, and Thanksgiving

The days grew shorter, and colder, too. Leaves were blown off the trees by winds that whistled at the windows and doors of the farmhouse, and blew cold into the barn, especially at night. Missus and Sadie emptied the garden of everything good, and then Mister used the rototiller to turn the soil, plowing under all the stalks and leaves that remained, so they would rot and enrich the soil for next year's garden.

When the garden had been emptied and the air had become bitter cold, Missus worked on her quilt, sitting in her chair in the living room. Sadie stayed with her to help. Unless there was a rainstorm, Angus and Mister went out, sometimes to plow the fields, sometimes to burn the piles of brush they had gathered, sometimes to check the fences.

One sunny, cold day, Missus and Sadie gave Mister and Angus a ride in the truck up to the summer sheep pasture. Mister and Angus got out to find the sheep and bring them all back to the pasture they had left in the spring. "Sheep want a more protected pasture in fall," Mister explained to Angus. "Fall weather can get rough." For that job, Angus had to be on the leash.

Even though it was colder, they still had training, three times each day. Sadie sometimes remembered the commands and sometimes obeyed, but Angus could remember and obey most of the time.

All of the time was what Mister wanted, so Angus wanted that, too. Angus knew that if he just worked harder, he would be able to get it right all of the time. He worked as hard as he could to remember everything, the commands he already knew—Sit! Come! Stay!, and Heel!—and the new one they were learning, Down! He tried his best, three times a day, every day. He liked doing it right. He liked making Mister happy. Sadie wanted to remember, too, but a lot of the time she couldn't. But she didn't worry. She did what she could and hoped training would be over with soon so she could get back to doing what she liked, which was sitting with Mister and Missus in the living room, or checking the pastures and barns and chicken houses with Angus, or napping in the kitchen with Patches, smelling all the good food smells.

One cold day, a great variety of smells spread from the kitchen throughout the whole inside of the house, all the rooms downstairs and upstairs, too. Missus spent all that day in the kitchen, and Patches spent all day on the windowsill, napping. Sadie couldn't stay in one place that long, so she came and went, smelling all the sweet fruity smells, mixed in with the warm bready smells and sharp onion smells.

The next morning, Missus added another smell, richer than any of the previous ones. "The turkey is stuffed and in the oven," she reported to Mister at breakfast.

"I can smell it," he said. "It smells great."

Angus and Sadie hadn't known that Mister could smell, too.

That day, Mister didn't leave the house to work in the fields, or the barn, except to take care of the cows and train the dogs. While Missus cooked, he worked briefly with Sadie, practicing Sit! and Stay! But he had Angus do everything, over and over. "My brother's bringing Lucy this afternoon," he said to Angus. "Lucy'll give you some real competition. She's already been in a trial. So you better look sharp."

What's a trial, do you know?

Not yet. I'll ask Lucy.

Who's Lucy?

She's competition.

What's competition?

It's a trial.

After training, Mister went inside to help Missus put plates and silverware out on the big dining room table, and napkins and glasses, too, walking back and forth from the kitchen to the dining room. Angus and Sadie followed him, to help, too.

"I like Thanksgiving," Mister said. "I may even like it better than Christmas."

"What are you giving thanks for this year?" Missus asked.

"For you, and our life together here. As usual."

"Me, too, but what else? I'm giving thanks for those four healthy lambs."

"Well, I guess I'm giving thanks for how trainable Angus is. He'll take a little of the wind out of my brother's sails, the way he's always boasting about Lucy. And for Sadie, too. Just for being herself."

What are thanks? Sadie wondered.

Angus didn't know. *They're things you give.*

But I didn't see anything.

You can't see them. They're things you give that you can't see.

"I'm giving thanks for having a friend around the house all day," Missus said, and bent down to rub Sadie's neck. "And for you, too, Angus. You're a friend, too."

"What about me, aren't I your friend?" Mister asked, and he laughed, and she laughed, too.

In the afternoon, three cars arrived, all filled with brothers and sisters. One of the brothers brought his dog, who was named Lucy. The brothers and sisters brought children, too, and one brought a baby in its own special basket.

When all of those people came into the house, Patches didn't hesitate for one second. He ran upstairs to a bedroom, jumped onto the bed, curled up on the pillow, and went to sleep.

Downstairs, everybody was taking off their coats and hanging them up on hooks in the mudroom. They were talking about how good the house smelled and how nice everyone looked and how glad they were to see one another again. The children ran around and around, going outside and then coming back inside to call, "I touched the cow!"

A sister called back. "Don't touch the cow! I told you not to touch the cow!"

Missus said, "It's all right. She can't hurt a cow."

"But a cow could hurt her."

"The cat scratched me! Twice!"

"What cat? Are those barn cats feral?"

"All the cats have annual shots and checkups. It'll be all right. We'll wash it off with hydrogen peroxide. Okay, sweetie?"

"Yes! And a bandage! Two bandages!"

Mister said to a brother, "So, are you going to show me what your famous Lucy can do this year? And I'll show you Angus? I'd like to see how they stack up against each other."

"Absolutely," the brother said. "But you have to remember that Lucy's eighteen months old. That's a big advantage, plus she has experience in a trial. So don't get upset if your dog can't keep up with her. He's not even a year yet, is he?"

"Almost," Mister said. "Eleven months, he's about full-sized now. Let's take the dogs outside. That'll also calm things down in here. Sadie, Angus, Come!" he said.

"Lucy, Heel!" the brother said, even though she was already at his side, a dog no bigger than Angus. She hadn't said hello, or explored the kitchen, or done anything other than stay right beside the brother, watching him.

I can Heel! *and* Down!, Lucy told Angus. Sadie trailed them out the door, and some of the children trailed behind Sadie.

I can stay for a long down, Lucy said. *What about you?*

I'm going to the trials in the spring, and I went to one this fall, and I already have one leg.

What's a leg? Angus asked.

Sadie said, *You already have four legs.*

Lucy paid no attention to Sadie. *Don't you know anything?* Lucy asked Angus. *When you go to a trial and you can obey, the judge gives you a leg.*

I had a broken leg, and they fixed it.

Why do you keep interrupting us? Lucy asked.

I'm not. Am I?

Outside, the two men gave orders to their dogs. "Down! Stay!"

All three dogs flattened themselves down onto the ground, and stayed there. Lucy and Angus were side by side, but Sadie was a little apart and behind them.

I worked with sheep once, Lucy said to Angus. *Probably, you haven't done that yet.*

This farm has its own herd of sheep, Angus answered.

The two men pretended not to remember the dogs. Instead, they talked to each other.

"Maturity counts," the brother said. "How does Angus do with standing for examination?"

"I don't know," Mister answered. "We'll try him, shall we?"

"Because some dogs don't like strangers handling them. Some dogs growl or snap at the judges. Or they move away and break the pose. That's an automatic disqualification."

"I bet Angus can do it, although I'm not so sure about Sadie."

"She'd growl? Would she bite?"

Mister laughed. "Sadie bite? You've got to be kidding. She'd never do that. She'd just back away. Either that or she'd sneak up close to the judge so he could pet her."

"A lot of the judges are women," the brother said.

"You know what I mean," Mister said. "Do you want to say hello to Bethie and Annie?"

They walked over to the cow pen, but every now and then they turned their heads to be sure the dogs were staying down.

The sky was low and heavy with gray clouds, and the air tasted cold. A wind blew through the bare tree branches, combing through the dogs' new thick coats, winding around the house and barn with a rushing sound, like water.

The three dogs lay still, watching the two men, waiting. From the house, they could hear voices talking and the wailing of the baby. They could see and hear the two men, who pretended they weren't keeping an eye on the dogs.

Snake strolled out of the barn with Fox behind him, and they also pretended not to see the dogs.

Are those your cats?

Them? They're just barn cats.

Ours is a house cat. Patches. He went upstairs.

Snake and Fox sauntered over toward the empty garden and then strolled back behind the three dogs. They were talking about the cold day, and the colder nights. They compared how thick their fur was, complimenting each other.

No, Snake, yours is much thicker.

But your undercoat has come in more evenly. You're the lucky one, Fox.

The dogs didn't move, but they cocked one ear apiece to hear where the cats were, and what they might be getting up to. None of them much trusted cats, especially barn cats.

Snake strolled closer to the dogs. Fox followed. A few feet away from the dogs' noses, the two cats came to a halt. They arched their backs, and hissed. Their tails, which they stuck straight up in the air, got thicker.

Lucy growled, low in her throat. *Stay off me.*

Or what? Snake sneered and Fox sneered, too. *Yeah, or what?* But they backed away from Lucy.

The two men turned to watch.

You feel like scaring ourselves some dogs? Snake asked Fox.

We could start with Sadie, Snake suggested, and took

two steps closer to Sadie.

Sadie stayed down, but she backed away.

We could start by both jumping on Sadie, Fox agreed, also taking two steps closer to her, and then two more. She pulled back her mouth and hissed through her teeth.

At the same time, Snake jumped high into the air with his legs out and claws unsheathed.

Sadie jumped up, wheeled around, and fled back to the house and up the steps. At the kitchen door, she barked and barked. She heard Mister calling her, but she didn't stop. She heard Lucy ask, *She isn't afraid of cats, is she?* Angus answered, as if embarrassed, *She's afraid of everything.* And she heard Snake and Fox, screeching in what would have been laughter if cats could laugh.

Then Missus opened the door. "What is it, Sadie? Whatever it is, it's all right now. You're with me now. Everything's all right."

But everything wasn't all right. Angus was saying that

she was afraid of everything, and she wasn't, and Lucy wouldn't talk to her, and there were children all over her house. Two of those children came right up to Sadie and grabbed at her.

"Doggie! Doggie!"

"I'm petting a dog!"

"Be gentle, sweetie. You don't want to frighten her."

The children hung over Sadie so heavy that her legs almost went flat on the floor.

"Mommy! Look! I'm riding the dog."

"Be nice now."

One of the children tried to stick her fingers into Sadie's mouth.

Sadie knew she couldn't snap at children, and she couldn't bite them. Nobody had told her that, she just knew it. She thought that probably, also, she shouldn't growl at them. She was pretty sure she wasn't supposed to scare children.

But *they* were scaring her, and they wouldn't stop. They wouldn't go away, either. Sadie couldn't get away from them. So she barked. *Help! Missus!*

"Quiet, Sadie," Missus called from the dining room.

Help! she barked again. *They're—*

But now the child who had poked her fingers into Sadie's mouth was crying, and all the others were going away. Sadie didn't wait for whatever those children might get up to next. She ran into the living room and hid behind the carrier in which the baby slept, where there was just enough room for her. She thought that maybe no child could see her when she was behind the baby, with her head down on her paws. The baby smelled milky and powdery, and those smells made Sadie feel quiet and safe again. She decided to stay with the baby, never mind all the excited voices and good smells coming from the kitchen.

After a while, Sadie heard the men and the dogs come back into the house, and a while after that Angus came to find her.

What are you doing? We've been standing for examination. Lucy knows a lot, more even than me. Come into the kitchen with us, Sadie.

Sadie didn't want to go anywhere.

What's the matter?

The children.

They're only children, they can't hurt. Not like cats. Why are you afraid of them?

I'm not afraid, I just don't like them. I'm not like you.

You have to try.

I do.

You have to try harder. Come back into the kitchen with me.

Sadie didn't want to. She knew that Missus and Mister were in there, too, and she wanted to be where Missus and Mister were. But the children were in the kitchen, too, and she couldn't tell what children would do.

Angus said, *Come on, Sadie.*

Sadie obeyed.

She obeyed, but she didn't like it in the kitchen, where everybody was moving around and she didn't know where a child might go next.

There's nothing to be afraid of, Angus told her.

They poke.

She's afraid of children? Lucy asked. *Why would any-body be afraid of children?*

They poke, Sadie said again, but the others weren't listening.

Later, in the dining room, everybody sat in chairs at the table, and nobody even noticed the dogs, who stayed under the table, napping, while everybody ate and talked. After that, as a special treat, Mister turned out the lights in the dining room, and Missus made the round, flat light move around on the floor.

When Sadie saw that light, she came out from under the table to try to touch it with her paws. When she chased the light, they all laughed, the men low and round, the children squeaky, and the women softly, with clapping. Because she was trying to get a paw on the light, Sadie barely noticed when one of the children came to try and help her catch it. When at last they turned on the big lights that made the little round light go away, the child started to cry, so Sadie went up to lick his face to help him feel better. *The light'll come back sometime,* she told the child. *It comes back.* The child's face tasted salty, and good, so she licked again. And then the child laughed, and so did everybody else again. It turned out that when she was licking his face and he was laughing, Sadie didn't mind that child.

First, they all washed the dishes, and then all the guests left with their children and Lucy, too. "Thank you," they said. "It was delicious. Thank you. Will you come to our house next year?"

Lucy told Angus, *I can show you some things next time. But don't bring Sadie.*

Mister and Missus, Angus and Sadie stood on the porch and watched as the cars drove down the long driveway and away. Then they all stood together on the porch in the quiet darkness for a little while longer.

"That was a good Thanksgiving," Mister said.

"It was a good dinner," Missus said.

"Angus isn't very much behind Lucy at all," Mister reported. "Even if my brother did hire her a professional trainer."

"You *did* have a good Thanksgiving, didn't you?" Missus laughed.

Later, when Angus and Sadie were alone in their stall, he told her, *When you do that, with dancing, and they laugh, they're laughing at you.*

I like it when they're laughing, Sadie said.

I don't, Angus told her. *And you shouldn't.*

Sadie didn't agree about that, so she didn't say anything.

Angus didn't notice.

8
How it's snow, not Snowing, and then Christmas

A few days after Thanksgiving, when Angus and Mister had been gone all afternoon doing something about the fences, Missus looked up from the piece of quilt she was sewing. She went over to the window and said, "Well, well. It's about time." Then she went through the kitchen and out onto the porch, putting on her coat, then down into the yard. Sadie followed. "It's snowing," Missus said.

Sadie looked around to see Snowing, but no one was there. The air was cold and full of floating things.

"Look, Sadie," said Missus. She put her hand out to catch some of the floating things, so Sadie knew that they were Snowing.

"Now it's officially winter," Missus said, sounding glad.

Was it Snowing or Winter, the floating things? Sadie wondered. Could it be both?

"What do you think of that?" Missus asked.

Snowing! Sadie barked. *Winter!* She didn't care which it was.

Missus laughed. "We'll have hot chocolate to celebrate. Snow and hot chocolate go together. You watch, those two will be back here in no time at—"

Angus and Mister were walking through the Snowing, coming up to the house from the barn. "Did you see this?" Mister called.

"I'm making hot chocolate!" Missus called back.

This is wet, Angus said, as he ran up onto the porch. *It doesn't look like rain, but it is.*

It's not rain, it's Snowing, Sadie told him. Then, because she wasn't sure and didn't want to pretend she knew something she didn't, she said, *Either that or it's Winter.*

The Snowing stayed in the air all afternoon, so that by the time Mister and Missus walked the dogs down to the barn after supper, it had piled itself up on the ground. The dogs stuck their noses into it.

Cold!

Cold!

Run!

Mister bent over to pick up a handful of Snowing, and he threw it far out ahead of him. "Fetch, Angus," he said, so Angus went running off to find it, where it had landed in the garden.

But it wasn't there. Angus sniffed and sniffed, but he couldn't find it.

So Mister threw another.

Angus ran to catch it in his mouth before it hid itself away on the Snowing-covered ground, but he was too late.

Then Missus bent down to pick up some Snowing, but instead of throwing it to Angus, she threw it at Mister. "You fetch," she said.

"Hey!" he said, and threw some right back at her.

"Hey, yourself!" She laughed. "You shouldn't tease Angus that way. Or any way. Or any dog."

"Okay," Mister said. "You're right. Angus, Come! I want to show you something."

Angus came, and Mister gave him the Snowing instead of letting him fetch it, and that wasn't nearly as much fun. When Angus took the Snowing into his mouth, it was cold. Not only that, but Angus didn't have it in his mouth for very long at all before it turned into water.

It's just water, he told Sadie.

No, it's Snowing, she told him.

Try eating it, he advised her.

So she did. *What happened to the Snowing? It's water!* she said.

I shouldn't tease you that way, Angus said.

By the middle of the next day, the Snowing had entirely disappeared. But before long, there was more of it floating down through the air. This new Snowing covered everything, just like the first time, but this one didn't go away the next day. Mister said, "The dogs had better move inside for the winter, don't you think?"

"I think so," said Missus.

So Angus and Sadie's blanket was folded up into a bed, which was moved to an empty kitchen corner. Their food and water bowls were also moved inside. Angus worried, *What about the barn? Who will take care of the barn?*

Inside is warmer, Sadie said. *It's close to Mister and Missus. You can take care of them instead. I can help.* She liked spending the long nights warm in the house, with Mister and Missus, Patches and Angus, all of them together.

Angus also liked the warmth of the kitchen at night, especially after the day he and Mister brought the sheep down to their pen behind the barn. That day, Angus started out cold, and he ended up cold and wet and tired. The sheep didn't go inside the barn to sleep, like the cows and cats. They had their own fenced pen behind the barn, with their own small three-sided house to stay in during bad weather. Angus thought that was a good place for the sheep in winter, but for some reason they were reluctant to come down from the snow-covered pasture. It made no sense to Angus, the way the sheep scattered off and tried to hide from Mister. Mister made whistling noises and waved his arms—"Sheep! Sheep! Hoo-eee!"—but the sheep didn't cooperate. They drifted apart, going nowhere, or they ran off into a far corner of the pasture. They were much worse at obeying than Sadie was. Getting them all from their pasture back to their pen was cold, hard work. After that long day, Angus was especially glad to eat a big dinner and then curl up on his blanket on the floor of the warm kitchen.

The next day, after midday training, when Mister called, "Let's go, Angus," Angus wasn't sure he wanted to go. He remembered how cold and tired he could get, going off with Mister to work. But Mister insisted, and he called to Sadie, too, "Let's go, Sadie," and then he called to Missus, "Let's go, honey." They all four went walking off together. They walked through the snow along the dirt road, and then they turned into the woods. Mister pulled a sled behind him.

In the woods, Mister sawed at the trunk of a fir tree while Missus held the tree upright, and Angus chased

Sadie through the Snowing. Then, Mister and Missus lay the tree on top of the sled and tied it on. Together they dragged it all the way back to the house.

"I wonder if we could train the dogs to pull in harness?" Mister said, as he pulled.

"They're herding dogs, not huskies," Missus said.

"I bet Angus could do it," Mister said.

When they got home, Mister and Missus took the fir tree inside and stood it up in the living room, away from the fire, near a window. Then they hung things on it, strings of lights and popcorn, balls that Angus wasn't allowed to chase, and other small toys he wasn't allowed to chew. The two dogs lay beside the fire and watched this strange behavior, wondering, until finally Missus explained, "This is a Christmas tree, Sadie. We always have a tree for Christmas."

"*And* we always have a rib roast," Mister said. "For Christmas dinner. Wait'll you smell *that*, Angus. Wait until you get a smell of Christmas dinner."

It didn't take the dogs long to learn that it was called snow, not Snowing. "It looks like we got a lot of snow last night," Mister said, looking out the kitchen window. "Maybe twelve inches, maybe sixteen. What do you think?"

"I think we're going to have a white Christmas," Missus said, opening the door to let Sadie and Angus out. "Let's see how the dogs like snow when it gets deep."

They said snow. Not Snowing. You told me the wrong thing, said Angus, who cared about being right.

Now we know, answered Sadie, who didn't.

"Come on, dogs!" Missus called. "Out!"

They ran together through the door and over the steps, to jump down onto the white ground. But they didn't land on the ground, they sank into it. They sank into it halfway up their legs.

Oh!

For a minute they stood stock still, too surprised to move.

What?!

The air was so bright that the dogs had trouble seeing, and it was icy, too. The snow was cold under their paws and up their legs. When they stuck their noses into the snow, it was so new, it had almost no smell at all. They chewed at it, but it melted into ice-cold water and drooled out of their mouths. This snow was so deep and cold and exciting, everything was so unlike it had been before, that the two dogs started to run—

But running in snow wasn't at all like running on the ground. You had to jump up for each step you ran forward, and each time you landed you had to sink in a little.

Missus watched them from the porch. "How do you like winter?" she asked.

Winter means snow and cold, Angus told Sadie.

Jump! she answered. *Play!* and she bumped right into him, knocking him over into the snow, biting at it and tossing it up into the air until Angus got back on his feet and bumped right into her, knocking her over into the snow. They liked winter just fine, especially since they could go into the warm house whenever they wanted.

Because of the cold and the snow, the other animals

kept close to the barn. The two cows stayed inside, except for when they went out to the cow pen where Mister kept their water and hay. Snake and Fox stayed up in the loft, catching mice and keeping warm in the piles of hay. Behind the barn, the sheep had their big pen, with a rail fence to keep them safe. They huddled in groups, or crowded together inside the three-sided shed where Mister put their food and water. In winter, their thick coats kept them warm. The chickens stayed in their house, and were—for chickens, who tend to be chatty—quiet.

Not long after that first deep snow, Mister and Missus set boxes under the lighted and decorated tree. They did this just before they went upstairs to bed. The next morning—as if they'd forgotten that they put the boxes there themselves—Mister and Missus took those same boxes out from under the tree and opened them. In one box they found marrow bones for Angus and Sadie to take outside and eat, and chew on, and bury.

The dogs had never had bones before. Everything kept being so different and so exciting—bones, and the snow, and Mister and Missus watching them from the kitchen door and laughing—that Angus pretended to fight with Sadie and Sadie pretended to fight back. Then they settled down on the packed snow by the porch steps, each holding a bone between their front paws, and chewing, as if they had bones all the time and already knew just what to do with them.

"Look at the two of them," Missus said.

"They know how to have a good time, don't they?" Mister asked. "Like children."

"Dogs make Christmas more fun," Missus said. "Like children would."

"Just look at them," Mister said.

"Do you ever think about having children?" Missus asked.

"Yes," Mister said. "I do."

That same day Mister and Missus had a big dinner, but no other people came to eat it, no children, and no other dogs, so it was perfect. They were entirely happy to be just them, just Mister and Missus, Angus and Sadie and Patches, and everywhere a smell that filled up their stomachs just smelling it.

That's what Mister was talking about, Angus reminded Sadie. *Rib roast.*

Christmas dinner, she remembered.

No, Angus corrected her. *He said rib roast.*

Even though it was just the two of them, Mister and Missus ate at the dining room table. When Missus sat down, she said to Mister, "Merry Christmas." When Mister gave Missus a plate of food, he said, "Rib roast makes the perfect Christmas dinner."

We were both right, Angus said. *But I was righter.*

How long does Christmas last? Sadie wondered. Angus didn't know. *Maybe always,* Sadie decided. *Maybe forever from now on.*

Patches knew better. *It goes away, I remember that. It goes away, and then, after a long, long time, it comes back.*

When will it end? Sadie wondered, but cats are no better than dogs at telling time.

When will they let us outside to chew on those bones again? That's what I want to know, Angus said.

Christmas went away, but winter stayed. The dogs got used to having icy snow on their paws when they came in from outside. They learned how to chew clumps of ice from them while they lay on their blanket in the warm kitchen. But if there was new snow on the ground—so fresh! so empty of any smell!—they were always eager to be outside. They barked, and ran, barking, through the snow. Once or twice, the snow was so deep that they sank in up to their shoulders.

Yikes!

Jump!

Up!

Oh!

When they had training and Mister or Missus said, "Down!" and then "Stay!," it was cold on their chests and bellies while they waited, and waited, and waited to hear "That'll do!" When they finally heard that command, they jumped up eagerly. Mister and Missus thought they were obeying, but really they were getting away from the freezing snow.

Day after day, the snow stayed on the ground. Sometimes the sky grew gray and cloudy, and even more snow fell. These conditions would have made training and running around impossible, if Mister hadn't used the pickup with its plow. The plow pushed snow away from the front of the barn and cleared the driveway, too. Missus shoveled the steps clear.

During winter, Mister and Missus stayed inside almost all of the time, fixing or making things or reading.

Sometimes Angus and Sadie stayed inside, too; but they also liked to go outside to check on the cows, to slip underneath the rails of the fence and make the sheep nervous, to sniff at the faint traces of scent left by the little creatures that came out at night, to eat whatever they might find in the snow-covered garden. Angus and Sadie had warm fur coats. They didn't want to stay inside most of the time. They wanted to be outside, running around in the snow, until they came in where it was warm, to eat and to sleep, until they could go outside again.

9
How it's Sadie who is the hero

One day, the sky hung especially low and dark over the farm, and a wind roared at the windows and doors of the house, and shoved against its walls, and howled all around the house and the barn.

"I'm doing a last check before this storm hits," Mister said. "I'll take the dogs because, if it's as bad as they say it's going to be, they won't get much exercise for a while."

"The snow's starting," Missus reported from the window. "It's not coming down heavy yet, but—wear your gloves."

"I am."

"And a scarf."

"I am."

"And a hat, too. With earflaps."

"I am, I am. Angus, Come! Sadie, Come!"

Sadie wasn't sure she wanted to step out into that wind. When she did, she wished right away that she hadn't. She hadn't known a wind could be that loud, or strong. She could barely walk through it. What really surprised her was how exciting it felt to be out in a storm. All the noise and confusion of a wind so hard it almost knocked her over made her heart race, and that made her want to bark and bark. Mister and Angus were there, so she knew she didn't have to be afraid.

They kept close together, all three of them. The wind pulled at the dogs' fur as it whirled past them, pushing their ears back against their heads. A few flakes of snow whipped into their faces. Angus lowered his tail, lowered his head, lowered his body, and followed behind Mister. Sadie, too, lowered her tail and head and body, and followed behind Angus. Inside the barn it was bitter cold, but the cows never noticed much except food and being milked. They mostly stood, and shifted on their hooves, and chewed. That was what cows did.

Mister pulled up his stool and milked Annie and Bethie, covering the two pails and setting them just outside the open doors of the barn. From their warm nests in the hay, the cats peered down at the two pails, but it was too cold and windy for them to think of leaving their loft to make a quick raid. "We'll pick these buckets up on our way back to the house," Mister was saying when—*Boom! Bash!*—there came a huge crashing sound, so big and heavy that even the wind couldn't drown it out. The cows looked up, worried. The cats burrowed for cover. Angus and Sadie looked at Mister, to find out what it was, but he was looking at them as if he expected them to know.

"What?!" Mister said.

I don't—

Is it dangerous?

"What was that?" Mister asked.

They all listened, but they didn't hear any more crashing. All they heard was the wind howling, just like before. Finally, Mister said, "That'll be bad news, I'll bet. Sounded like a tree's down. Luckily, it's not near the house, and it looks like it didn't get the barn roof, but I bet you dollars to doughnuts it scared the sheep."

Dollars?

Doughnuts?

"And they were probably already in a panic because of the storm. You know how jittery sheep are," Mister explained. He led the two dogs out of the barn, pulling the wide doors closed. "Sheep are bolters."

Snow was now blowing thick through the air.

"Let's go see what's what with the sheep," Mister called, loudly enough for Angus and Sadie to hear him through the wind as he headed off behind the barn.

Snow fell thickly onto Sadie and she had trouble keeping close to Angus, but she managed, even when they turned the corner and the wind really attacked them, blowing snow so hard into their faces that it was hard to keep their eyes open.

"Some storm, isn't it, Angus? What do you think of this weather, Sadie?" called Mister, but the wind grabbed his words and blew them away. Angus and Sadie barely heard him. They could barely see him to follow close on his heels as he walked around the sheep pen, with one hand on the top rail of the fence to guide him. His scent was quickly covered by the snow.

They arrived at a dark, high mass of branches where the wind had torn up a big pine tree, ripping its roots up out of the ground and throwing it onto the rail fence. The fallen tree had knocked down part of the fence, and there were sheep everywhere, scooting around the pen in groups of three and four. The sheep bolted back and forth in terror and panic, and two were running out through the break in the fence. No, three sheep were escaping. One sheep was way ahead of the other two.

"Hey! Hey!" Mister shouted. He ran toward the escaping sheep, waving his arms. Angus ran with him, barking, with Sadie behind.

Mister's loud voice, combined with Angus's barking, frightened the sheep even more.

When sheep are frightened, first they stop dead in their tracks. Then, they look down at the ground or around at one another, pretending there is nothing to be afraid of after all. Finally, suddenly, as if they've made a group decision, they break and run fast.

When Mister yelled, the two closest sheep stopped dead in their tracks long enough for him to catch up to them, but the third one had time to stop, and then to decide to run off.

"Hey!" Mister shouted at the two sheep. "Back! Go on now!" He waved his arms to drive them past the fallen tree, back into the pen. Angus stayed beside him to help, barking. "Good going, Angus," Mister said, waving his arms and yelling. "Hey now! *Hoo-eee*, sheep!"

There's one more, Sadie said.

I know. I'll take care of it.

It's bolted off into the woods.

I know. Just wait until I'm through here.

But Sadie didn't wait. That sheep was already out of sight in the trees. It was going to get itself lost. Sadie took off after it. Behind her, she heard Mister call, "Sadie, Come! Sadie, Sit!" But she had a sheep to go after.

The sheep's track was only a faint smell that was already fading away under the fast-falling snow, so Sadie put her head down and ran as fast as she could, following the track through the trees. In the trees the sound of the wind wasn't so loud and the snow wasn't so deep. After a little while, Sadie had come close enough to hear the sound of the sheep running away. The sound was muffled by the snow and buried in the wind, but it was still just loud enough to hear, and to follow. Sadie had to pay very close attention so as not to lose track of the sheep.

She followed and followed, without thinking of

where she was going and where she had been. It was darker in the woods than in the fields, but Sadie knew what she was doing: She was following that sheep, to find it for Mister. She didn't worry about the trees all around her or the snow coming down thick through the air. She worried about finding that sheep.

When she finally caught up with it, it was leaning against a big tree, shaking. Its eyes were closed tight. Sadie barked once, not very loudly, and the sheep's eyes opened. Sadie dropped down onto the ground, and eyed the sheep.

That sheep was frightened of her! It was so frightened that it just closed its eyes, to pretend she wasn't there, to pretend it wasn't tired and lost and cold and all alone, to pretend everything was all right. Sadie understood how that sheep was feeling. She said, *I'm here now*, the way Missus did. *Everything's all right now*. The sheep couldn't understand her, but that didn't matter. *Mister will be here any minute*, she told the sheep, and then she settled down on the ground to wait, as if she had been ordered to Down! and Stay! and she was obeying. She settled down with her eyes fixed on the sheep.

But Mister didn't come, and neither did Angus. Sadie waited and waited, and they still didn't come. The air got darker, the snow kept on falling, she was getting too cold, and they still didn't come.

Where were they?

The wind howled around her ears. It was so loud, she almost couldn't even hear her own thinking.

When would they come?

She knew they would be angry at her for not obeying, but she still wanted them to come.

Why hadn't they caught up with her by now?

The wind howled and howled, as if that was the answer to her question, and Sadie began to worry that Mister and Angus might be lost in the woods, in the storm.

What if they couldn't find her? What if they never found her?

At that thought, Sadie stood up. She shook herself free of all the snow that had piled up on her while she was waiting. Now *she* was afraid.

Angus had told her over and over that she was afraid, and she had worried that he might be right, even though she didn't agree with him. Now she knew for sure that Angus had been wrong. Now that she really was afraid, she knew just how dark and cold and lonely fear felt.

She was as frightened as the sheep now, because she knew the wind would keep on howling, and it would get colder and colder, and there would be more and more snow. She didn't know what would happen then, but she knew it wouldn't be anything good. Nothing warm, for example, nothing with food, nothing like being at home in the kitchen with Missus and Patches and waiting for Angus and Mister to come in from the barn. After colder and colder came something bad. She wasn't sure exactly what, but she was very sure about bad.

These thoughts made Sadie even more afraid. She wished she had obeyed Angus and waited for him. If she had waited for Angus, Angus would be here, and he would know what to do.

She wished she had obeyed Mister, and Come! when he had called. If she had done that, she wouldn't be here alone with this silly frightened sheep.

She was all alone, and she didn't know what to do, and that sheep just stood there with its eyes closed as if it were asleep in the shed beside the barn with the rest of its flock, as if nothing were wrong.

But everything was wrong.

They had to get home.

Sadie suddenly knew that, for sure. She didn't know where home was, or what was the way from here to home, but she did know that one thing, *Home.*

At that thought—but it wasn't a thought, it was a feeling, a sense of where Missus was, as if she could smell the kitchen—Sadie's legs knew where to go.

But how could she know if her legs were right?

If Angus were here, he'd know the way and she could

follow him. It was so cold and the wind was so loud, and
the branches of the trees were waving in the darkness all
around, and the snow kept falling and kept falling. . . .
Sadie wished for Angus so hard that she had to howl.
And howl.

The wind took her howls up and blew them away,
and they were lost in the thick falling snow. So she
stopped howling.

Sadie shook herself again, to shake off the new snow
from her coat and to shake out the howling feeling inside
her. Even if she couldn't find her way home, she was

going to have to do it, because Angus wasn't here. Here, Sadie was the only one who could do anything.

She turned to go off in the direction her legs wanted. But then she remembered the sheep, because that sheep was her work. You couldn't just walk away from your work. If Angus were here, he would bring the sheep home with him. Sadie knew that.

Sadie went up to the sheep where it was leaning against the trunk of the tree with closed eyes. She barked right into its face.

The eyes stayed closed.

She barked again, and growled as if she were Snake or Fox, about to attack.

The eyes flew open, and the sheep stared at her out of wide wild eyes.

Home, she told it. *We have to go home.* She dropped down flat on the ground and eyed the sheep.

After staring at her for a minute, the sheep turned and jumped off sideways, about to bolt off.

About to bolt off in the wrong direction.

Sadie jumped up and got in its way. She dropped down and eyed it again. The sheep stopped, standing with the snow halfway up its thin legs. Sadie tried to know what to do.

What would Angus do?

She didn't know. Sadie wasn't Angus—how could she know what he'd do?

The sheep started to move away from her in another wrong direction, and then Sadie figured it out: If she was standing in the wrong direction, the sheep would bolt off in the right direction.

But there were so many wrong directions to block off.

She was getting colder, and it was almost as dark as night, and the snow kept on falling and the wind kept on blowing. So Sadie did the only thing she could. She ran around behind the sheep, lowered her head, and growled.

The sheep ran off for a little bit, in almost the right

direction, and then stopped to stare at her, frightened.

Sadie moved a little to one side and eyed it. The sheep moved again and stopped again.

That sheep didn't want to go through the snow. It wanted to stop under trees. It was frightened by the loud howling wind. It wanted Sadie to go away and leave it alone.

Again and again, that sheep moved, and then stopped. Again and again, Sadie growled or barked, and then fell to the ground and eyed it. Twice, the sheep tried a quick sideways turn, a bolt of speed to get away from her. It was as if that silly sheep *wanted* to be lost, and *wanted* to get colder and colder, until whatever worst that could happen had happened.

Instead of going home, which was what Sadie wanted.

Sadie ran around the sheep and made it turn around and take a few more steps toward home.

It was a long, dark, cold, and windy time before Sadie drove the sheep out of the woods. Beyond the protection of the trees, snow blew into her eyes, her nose, and her ears. It had piled up on the ground as deep as her chest. But Sadie knew where she was. She was home!

Or, almost home. She knew exactly where home was now, and it was close. Sadie plowed forward. The snow didn't matter anymore. It didn't matter how cold she was because soon she would be warm, and Missus would give her something to eat, and Mister wouldn't be angry when he saw the sheep, and Angus would be proud of her.

For about ten steps—ten leaps, really, through the deep snow, ten happy, excited leaps—Sadie moved forward. Then she stopped, because the sheep had already turned around and was trying to run back through the snow on its spindly legs, back into the woods where the snow wasn't so deep and the wind didn't blow so hard. The sheep didn't know how close they were to home.

Sadie didn't have to take care of that sheep. Nobody had told her to, not Mister and not Angus. She didn't want to take care of it, either. But she turned around and leaped after it. She didn't bark until she had drawn ahead of it, so that her barking would stop it. After it stopped, she barked again, and it turned to get away from her. That silly sheep didn't even know it was going home.

When they got to the barn and the sheep heard its flock, it stopped again. This time Sadie left it where it was, standing up against the fence. It didn't remember where the break in the fence was, so it stayed fenced out, calling in a high, whiny voice to the other sheep to let it in, to come join it. Sadie didn't wait. She ran around the barn and up the steps to the porch. She stood at the door in the howling wind and blowing snow, and barked.

Nobody opened the door. What if they couldn't hear her? What if they were upstairs in bed? Sadie barked again, twice, and that time, Angus barked back from inside. *Sadie?*

Then the kitchen door opened, and Missus was kneeling to let Sadie climb onto her lap.

"You're safe," Missus said.

You shouldn't have run off like that, Sadie.

"You certainly had us worried," Mister said. "This is a real blizzard. Didn't you hear me calling you?"

I didn't think you'd be able to find your way back.

That sheep is beside the pen.

"She must be starving," Missus said. She stood up. "And I'll towel you dry, too. What were you doing running off? And you might as well get away from the door, I'm not letting you back outside."

The pen behind the barn? Okay, I'll take care of it.

"Now what's got into Angus?" Mister said. "All right, boy, I hear you. Is something going on outside? I guess I'd better—all right, good dog, I'm coming. Sadie, you stay. Angus and I will take care of this. Just give me a chance to get my boots on, Angus."

By the time Sadie had eaten and been toweled dry and was about to fall asleep—which wasn't very long at all— Mister and Angus had returned.

Mister was amazed, and proud. "She brought it back, honey. That's why it's been so long. I can only imagine how much trouble that sheep gave her. Good girl, Sadie. You're a real hero."

Missus, too, was amazed and proud. "I didn't know you could be so brave. And clever, too, to herd a sheep in a storm. You really are a wonder, Sadie, aren't you?"

Sadie was so sleepy, she almost couldn't enjoy all the praise.

You should have waited for me, Angus said. *With two of us, it wouldn't have taken so long, and they wouldn't have had to worry so much. I told you to wait,* he reminded her.

But Sadie was asleep and didn't hear.

10
How Angus feels
when Sadie is the hero

Sadie wanted to tell Angus about it. *When I was alone, with the sheep but alone, and it was the storm,* she began.

Later, Angus said. *I'm busy.*

Angus had his work to do with Mister, and he didn't want to be distracted. He didn't want to be disturbed. So when Sadie said, *After I found the sheep I waited—,* Angus said, *Not now. Can't you see I'm doing something important?* At night when Sadie asked, *Can I tell you now?* Angus interrupted, *No. I'm tired. I worked hard all day, Sadie.*

After a few days, Sadie stopped trying to tell him about it, as if she had forgotten, which she probably had,

Angus thought. Sadie wasn't very good at remembering things. Angus knew that; they all knew that.

She wasn't the only one who wasn't good at remembering things, thought Angus. Mister and Missus seemed to have forgotten all about how Sadie didn't obey. She had gone running off into the storm, disobeying Mister, just like she had gone running off after that skunk. Nobody had praised Sadie for disobeying then. Just the opposite. Angus remembered that. But now Mister and Missus talked about what a wonder Sadie was for running off after a sheep. It was as if Angus had never gone to find a sheep in the woods, as if Sadie's sheep was ten times more important than the one Angus had found in the woods, or even the two Angus had helped Mister get back into the pen during the storm.

Angus didn't see what was so wonderful about Sadie's one sheep, when he had helped save two. Three, if you counted the first.

There was one good thing about all this, however, which was that now Sadie would have to start being braver, and better at being obedient, too. Angus could help her learn that. Everybody preferred a brave and well-trained dog, and everybody respected that dog more. He would help Sadie be more respected. He decided to do that, and he decided they would start with the cats.

The days were getting longer and warmer, even though the snow hadn't all melted away. During the days, Mister opened the barn doors to let the sun heat the inside. That meant the dogs could go into the barn by themselves. *Come on,* Angus said to Sadie one sunny day.

Where?

Just come on.

Angus headed for the open barn door, with Sadie trailing. He went along beside the garden and down the path. Sadie followed.

Inside the barn, Angus made one complete tour, taking his time, smelling everything he felt like smelling, ignoring the cats, who watched from underneath the tractor. Sadie kept close behind him.

The cats are under the tractor, she reported. *Watching.*

You have to stop being afraid of those cats.

It's not afraid. Not really afraid. In the storm, in the woods—

Not now. I'm busy checking this out.

Angus started on a second slow tour of the barn, walking through sunlight, walking through shade. This was his barn. He was in charge of this barn. Any cat that might happen to be watching could see that. He was in charge of Sadie, too. He walked all around the inside of the barn, slowly, with Sadie still following him, and then, slowly, slowly, he went back out through the open doors.

Behind him, Sadie yelped.

Angus wheeled around, barking at the cats, warning them. *Back off!*

Fox, who had run out from under the tractor to jump onto Sadie's back, fled up the ladder into the loft. Sadie ran to stand close behind Angus.

Do something, Angus told her. He didn't care how frightened she might be, he was going to make her learn to be brave. *So they'll know you're not afraid of them.*

But I don't think I am. Not afraid, not really afraid.

Angus lost patience. *I'll show you how.* Snake was still under the tractor, so Angus ran right at it, as if when he got there he was going to crawl under it to catch Snake in his teeth, and bite him and shake him. Snake scooted out the opposite side, across the barn floor, and up into the loft.

See? Angus asked, going back outside to join Sadie. *See how easy it is?*

Yes, Sadie answered. Then she admitted, *No. I mean not easy. Not for me.*

Angus said, *You have to learn how. That's why I'm helping you.*

Oh. All right. But—

If I'm helping, you should say thank you.

Oh. Thank you.

A couple of days later, Angus tried again. Once more he led Sadie down to the barn. *What if they jump at me?* she asked.

Let them try it, Angus said. *Just let them try it.*

The two dogs walked into the barn and into the shadows. They walked around and around, Sadie just behind Angus, and the cats never made a sound, and they never made a move either.

They're up in the loft, Sadie said.

Don't be afraid.

Sadie thought about it. *I'm not.*

Good girl, Sadie, said Angus, just like Mister. *Now, I want you to walk around once without me. Just once, that's all. That's not very hard,* he said, as if she had said she didn't want to do it.

In order to keep Angus near as long as possible, Sadie started her round before Angus had gone out the barn doors. She walked all around the inside, starting at the cow stalls and going along behind the tractor. She came to the stall where she and Angus slept in warmer weather. Their stall came just before the steps to the loft, and then there were just two more stalls with farm and garden tools in them, and a storeroom door before she got back to the big open doorway and the bright warm sunlight—

Something jumped at her, from out of a stall where

hoes and rakes and shovels were kept leaning against the wall.

And something else jumped out at her, from out of the same stall. Shovels and rakes and hoes clattered onto the ground.

The two things screeched. They were jumping and screeching.

Sadie leaped up into the air, and she yelped, and she ran. It was only the cats. She knew it was only the cats. She knew it, but when they jumped at her she couldn't help yelping and running.

Angus asked, *What went wrong?*

Sadie explained. *They jumped.*

You shouldn't yelp. They like it when you yelp. That's why they jump at you.

I was trying not to.

You have to not yelp.

I can't, Sadie explained. *They jump, and I hear them, and I know what they're doing, and they screech that way. They're jumping AT me,* she explained.

Angus gave up. *Well, it's too bad about you. I can't do anything with you.* Then he tried to make her feel better. *I guess you'll never be able to stand up to the cats, so let's stop trying. Because you can't do it.* Now that that was settled, Angus felt better.

Sadie didn't feel better.

We can work on training instead, Angus promised her. *I can help you with obeying.*

All right, Sadie said, and then she remembered. *Thank you.*

Angus began this new project by helping Sadie only when they were inside the house, because he wanted to let her get used to him training her. So every now and then, when they were together in the house, he would tell her, *Sadie, Sit!*

It took her a while to learn to hear him saying that, but once she got the idea, Sadie started to obey him.

"Whatever are you doing, girl?" Missus asked. "I thought you wanted to go out." Sadie had been heading for the door Missus was holding open, but then— plunk—she sat down on the kitchen floor. Missus laughed. "Changed your mind? You are the world's silliest dog. Come here, and let me give your neck a nice scratch."

Sadie obeyed Missus, but Angus told her, *You're supposed to wait until I say That'll do! You should know that by now.*

I do know it. But Missus called me.

Next time, you have to wait until I release you. You have to practice or you'll never improve.

But you didn't say Stay! Mister says Sit! and Stay!

You're saying I'm doing it wrong?

No, not wrong. Just not right.

It turned out that being the trainer was harder than Angus had thought. He admired Mister all the more, once he understood how hard it was. When you were the trainer, you had to think about things more, and think about them sooner.

The next time he practiced training Sadie, Angus waited until they were alone in the kitchen, after Mister and Missus had gone upstairs to bed. *Sadie, Sit!* he said. *Stay!*

It took longer than Angus thought it should, but finally Sadie got up from where she was napping on the floor, and sat. Then she watched Angus, and waited. He was pleased with how well he was training her, and he made her wait just a little longer before he said, *That'll do!* As she sprang up, he added, *Good girl, Sadie.*

He liked being the trainer. He liked it so much, he stopped minding that Sadie had run off into the storm, and saved the sheep, and made everybody forget that he had saved sheep, too. It turned out that if she hadn't been disobedient, he wouldn't have known that he could train her himself.

After several days of this practice, Angus started to help Sadie when Mister was training them. He knew he understood her better than Mister did, because Mister wasn't another dog. He knew he also understood how Mister liked to train, because it was the way Angus liked to learn. Angus was sure he could help Sadie learn that way.

"Sadie, Down!" said Mister.

Sadie looked at Mister, and lay down.

Down! said Angus.

Sadie looked at Angus. She was already down.

"Stay!" said Mister.

She looked at Mister.

Stay! Sadie, you can do it, said Angus.

She looked at Angus. Did Angus think she couldn't do it? But she *was* doing it, wasn't she? But what if Angus was right and she couldn't do it? Was he right? Did Missus know what she should do?

"Why is she looking at you?" Mister asked Missus.

Sadie looked at Mister.

"She's not," Missus said.

Sadie looked at Missus.

You're getting distracted, said Angus. *Don't get distracted. I know how hard it is for you, but try a little harder.*

The more Angus told Sadie how hard it was, the harder it got for Sadie to remember and obey.

"You're having trouble today, girl," Mister said.

I'm here, said Angus. *I'm right with you. Not much longer—okay, Sadie, that's pretty good. That'll do!*

Sadie rose to her feet.

"Sadie, Down!" Mister said.

Sadie got down again.

"And Stay!" said Mister.

You'll do better next time, Angus said. *Don't feel too bad about it. It's really hard, I know. We can practice some more, later, just the two of us.*

But— Sadie started to say.

"That'll do!" Mister said.

Angus got up, and Sadie followed his example.

"What's got into you today?" Mister asked, as he bent down to rub gently on Sadie's ears.

Don't worry about it, Angus reassured her. *He's not really angry. He's just disappointed.*

As soon as Angus said that, Sadie really started to worry. She didn't want to be a disappointment to anybody. Of course, because she worried about it, she got worse at being trained.

The next day and the day after that, Sadie tried even harder when they were training, and Angus tried even harder to help her. He offered encouragement: *I know you're getting tired, but keep trying. I know how hard it is, but just a little bit more.*

"Sit!" Mister said. As soon as he said it, Angus would say *Sit!* Sometimes Angus got it wrong, and when Mister said "Come!," he said *Down!* Sadie tried to do it right. She started to *Come!*, but then she did *Down!* Then she understood that Angus meant to say *Come!* so she got up again and went to Mister.

"You are in a slump, Sadie," Mister said on the third day. "Have we been pushing you too hard? Let's slow down a little, and review. Sit!" he said.

Sadie sat.

"Stay!" Mister said.

Sadie stayed. Missus stayed with her. Mister went to work with Angus, practicing *Heel!* They walked down to the barn, slowly. Sometimes Mister stopped and Angus sat down, close beside his leg. As soon as Mister started walking again, Angus was up and moving along right behind his leg. When they got to the barn, they turned around to come back, Angus always at the same distance from Mister's leg.

"Good girl, Sadie," Mister called to her.

That'll do! Angus called.

Sadie got up. She took a few steps, then she realized Angus's error and sat again.

"Uh-oh," Mister said. "I didn't release you, Sadie. We

need to review *That'll do!*, don't we? Another day," he said, and she could see that he was disappointed. Again.

Sadie was disappointed, too. She had really liked it when Mister and Missus were so proud of her and thought she was a wonder. She wanted to have that good feeling again.

Angus didn't seem to mind when Sadie had trouble obeying Mister. Angus was very patient. But Sadie minded. She definitely did not like getting worse at training. She kept thinking about the cats, too.

Sadie had had an idea about the cats. She didn't like the idea, but she thought it was a good one. She didn't tell it to Angus, because she didn't want him getting his hopes up. She didn't want him being disappointed in her, too. But she kept thinking about her idea, which was: She could try it on her own, try learning to be brave about the cats without any help.

That idea meant going into the barn alone, and it took quite a few days for Sadie to find enough courage. She kept wanting to, and she even got started off down the path, but she wasn't able to make herself go right up to the barn, and then inside.

The days grew still longer, and the last of the snow had melted away. Every night Sadie decided that the next day would be the day she tried, but when that day came, she decided she had better wait for the next next one. It was easier to be brave, Sadie thought, when you didn't have any time to think about it. It was easier when you just ran off into the woods to rescue a sheep.

But this idea about going into the barn alone wasn't like that. You had to think about it, and then choose to do it, and then make yourself walk up to the barn—alone—and in through the big doors.

Sometimes, at night, in the safety of the kitchen, Sadie felt brave enough to promise herself that she would try. Usually, in the morning she was disappointed and impatient with herself because she kept putting it off and not doing it. She liked her nighttime feelings, but she couldn't make them last into the next day. She hated her daytime feelings and was glad when they went away at night.

And then one day . . .

Why that day? Maybe because the sun was warm. Maybe because Angus and Mister had taken the tractor off into the woods, so no one but Sadie would know if she failed. Maybe because that morning Sadie got more tired of being scared to try than she had ever been before. Or maybe because that morning—with the sun so warm and the sky so bright, how could anything bad happen on a day like that?—she really believed she could do it. Whatever the reason, or maybe for all of them put together, on that day Sadie could make herself try.

Besides, Missus was in the house if anything bad happened.

Having decided to try it, Sadie decided next that she wouldn't think one single thing about it anymore. She would just do it. Right away. So she walked down toward the barn.

She walked down to the barn and up to the open door.

She walked right through the door until she was where the sunshine turned into shade. Then she stopped.

The cats were inside. She heard them moving up in the hayloft, and then she heard them sneaking down the ladder.

Sadie wanted to turn and run away, but instead she took more steps, until she was all the way inside the barn. Without the tractor, there was one less thing for the cats to hide behind. She walked by the cows, sniffing, acting as if she was checking up on things, looking around as if she needed to be sure everything was all right, as if she was doing Angus's job while he was away, working.

She could hear the cats moving in the shadowy stalls across from her.

She was halfway around the barn, and she knew the cats were waiting. They were waiting to jump out at her. When they jumped, she would yelp and try to get away from them. She knew that, too. Angus said she shouldn't yelp, but she couldn't help it.

Sadie walked on, in the shadowy darkness, sniffing. She came to the empty stalls.

Hissing, Snake leaped out at her from the first stall. His claws were out, and Sadie saw his sharp, pointed teeth just before she yelped and jumped back. Then Fox leapt out at her from behind Snake, and Sadie yelped and jumped again. Her heart was beating in her throat, in her ears. All her hair stood on end. She could feel the hair on her neck and on her rump.

Sadie couldn't help it, she yelped again.

But she kept her own idea in her head, and after she yelped, she began to bark. It wasn't very loud barking, because it had to push past her heart to get out of her throat, but it was loud enough to sound like an angry dog. Her barking surprised the cats. They were waiting for her to run back to the house. They didn't know what to do, so they stood with arched backs and fat tails, and hissed some more.

Sadie barked again, and this time she also growled, low in her throat.

You want we should go for you again? Snake asked.

Sadie didn't even think of answering. She just did what she had decided to do. She closed her eyes and ran at the two cats, barking as loudly as she could. After a few steps, she stopped and opened her eyes.

At first, she couldn't see them at all. Then she did.

They had gone off in two directions, Snake up the ladder to the loft and Fox out the doorway into the sunlight. Once safely out of the barn, with all the outside to flee into, Fox stopped. She turned around.

As if she was attacking, Sadie ran right at Fox and barked again twice, loudly. Fox fled, running out of sight around the side of the barn. Snake stayed up in the safety of the high loft, not even looking down. With the cats taken care of, Sadie could step quietly out of the barn, into the sunlight and safety of the yard.

She pretended that she was just taking care of things, as usual, but her heart was still racing in her chest, and she worried that Snake would run down from his safe perch to jump at her, landing on her back and sticking his sharp claws into her. She knew she wasn't really brave, just pretending, but now she also knew what she could do about those cats. And something more, too.

She knew that Angus was wrong about being afraid. It didn't matter if she felt brave or felt frightened. What mattered was what she did about those feelings. Not everything was the way Angus said it was, and Angus didn't have to worry about her as much as he thought he did. Sadie couldn't wait for him to get home that evening, so she could tell him what she had done.

You what? Angus asked her, amazed. *That was really dumb, Sadie. You don't know cats like I do.*

But—

You were lucky to get away with it.

Angus didn't get it. Sadie tried again.

They ran away. When I barked and charged.

There must have been some other reason, Angus explained.

Sadie wasn't sure Angus could understand what she was telling him, so she stopped trying. It was almost as if he didn't want to understand that he had something wrong. But if he didn't understand, how could he change and get it right?

The next day when Missus was training them, and she had told them to "Sit!" and then "Stay!," Angus started to help Sadie again. *Take it easy. You can do it. I know you want to get going, but wait, wait just a little longer, Sadie. Just another breath, wait one breath. Good, now another . . .*

Sadie was getting confused again, and that made it harder for her to be trained. She wanted Angus not to help her anymore, especially right now. *That'll do! Angus,* Sadie said. She needed to pay close attention to Missus. She tried to explain that to Angus. *You don't know everything. That'll do!*

11

How everybody knows something but nobody knows everything, and it's not a race

When Sadie said to Angus, *You don't know everything,* Angus almost said right back, *I never said I did.* Because he never had. He was just better at things than she was, better at everything. They both knew that. But when Sadie told him *That'll do!* as if she was the trainer, that made Angus angry.

Angus had tried to help Sadie, and now all she had to say to him was *That'll do!* as if he was a pest. As if he *wanted* to spend all his time helping her. As if he'd never helped her at all. Thinking about it made him really angry.

It felt good to be angry at Sadie. Being angry cheered Angus up.

He figured that it wouldn't be very long before Sadie got scared by something, by the cats, or maybe some wind howling at a window, or even just the tractor being turned on. Something would frighten her and she'd come running.

But he wouldn't help her. Not anymore. He was done helping Sadie. Because she was acting as if he hadn't ever helped her at all. Telling him *That'll Do!* like that. Angus was good and angry now. He kept on being angry, day after day.

Sadie didn't notice this, not really. The days were warmer, as well as longer, and the snow had all melted away, so Angus and Mister went out into the woods to cut up the trees that had blown down in the winter storms. They were gone all day, and when they returned, Angus fell asleep almost right away. The dogs were over a year old now, and they got fed only once, in the mornings, so at night there was nothing to do except fall asleep. Sadie didn't have many chances to notice Angus being angry at her.

Everything was muddy: the driveway, the animal pens, the pastures. The dogs moved back to the barn for the nights, and the sheep—with two new lambs this year—moved back to the spring pasture. Angus and

Sadie were not allowed to go along for the move. "They've just learned not to go into the sheep pen," Mister said. "I don't want to ask too much of them. It's spring, and everybody's a little nutty in spring. Even Angus, aren't you, boy?" So Angus and Sadie stayed in the house that morning, Angus napping alone in the living room, not even answering when Sadie asked why didn't he come into the kitchen to drink some water and lie in the sunlight with her and Patches.

The air in spring was soft to breathe and warm with sunlight. It was the sweetest air of the whole year. But everybody was so busy—cleaning house and turning over the fields, planting seeds in trays full of tiny pots, clearing fallen trees and mending the fences—that nobody had time to appreciate the air. Nobody, that is, except Sadie, and Sadie had the time only because what little time there was for training was spent on Angus.

Mister wanted to take Angus to the trials in April. "My brother's had Lucy in trials twice already, last spring and last fall. Angus is at least as well-trained as Lucy was last spring, and he's probably smarter than she is."

"Maybe, but your brother had that professional trainer work with Lucy. That has to make a big difference."

"The trials are down in Massachusetts. I'd need to be gone a couple of days. Would you mind?"

"Not with Sadie for company. I can easily take care of

the cows, and if you turn the garden over before you go, I can make a good start on the planting."

"Are you sure you should be doing that kind of heavy work?" Mister asked.

"The stronger I am, the better it'll be for the baby," Missus said.

What baby? Sadie asked. *Angus, did you hear that?*

When Angus didn't answer, when he acted as if she hadn't said a thing, Sadie finally understood that something was wrong with him, and that what was wrong with him was probably her fault. She didn't know what she had done wrong, but it was obvious she had done something.

The dogs slept together in the barn, but it wasn't the same. They had their old blanket in their old stall, and the familiar barn noises around them, but everything had changed, because Angus and Sadie were different. They were like a dog and a cat—or a dog and a chicken, or even a dog and a cow—two entirely different kinds of animals that just happened to be living in the same stall. Two different kinds of animals do different kinds of things, and they especially don't do things together. That is the way it was with Angus and Sadie.

For example, when Angus patrolled around the inside of the barn at night, he didn't want Sadie to go with him. Sadie minded this, but she didn't say anything about it.

And on the first night the dogs had returned to the barn, the barn cats jumped at Sadie. She leaped up, yelping, but then she turned and barked at them, chasing them off, and she never asked Angus for help. Angus didn't say anything about that. Afterward, Snake and Fox left Sadie alone, and Angus didn't say anything about that, either.

Sometimes, Sadie heard a noise from the garden and went out alone to be sure everything was all right. Everything was always all right, and she thought that if there really did happen to be some animal there, a dangerous raccoon, or a fox, Angus would come to help her if she really needed it. So she wasn't too worried. It was worrying enough out in the dark garden, listening to hear if she was going to have to do something. But when she growled low in her throat, the animals were as frightened of her as she was of them, and they rustled away into the darkness. She didn't know what kind of animals they might be, and she couldn't ask Angus. He didn't want her asking him questions.

Angus was working particularly hard with Mister at training, getting ready for the trials. Often, Mister didn't really train Sadie at all. Angus watched silently while Mister had Sadie Sit! Down! Stay!, and Come!, just one time. Then Mister said, "That'll do!" and sent Sadie back to sit beside Missus so he could work with Angus. Angus almost never made any mistakes, no matter how many times Mister gave him an order. He was perfect, and Mister said so.

"Does he have to be perfect?" Missus asked.

"No, of course not," Mister said. "But it's nice if he is. Why? Do you have something against perfect?"

"No, I just have something against *having* to be perfect."

"Angus knows he doesn't have to be perfect."

"Do you really think so?" Missus asked.

"Besides, you're perfect, too," Mister said. "Perfect for me, I mean."

"Oh, you mean *that* kind of perfect? Well, yes, of course I am!" Missus said, and they laughed.

They could laugh, but Angus planned to be perfect, absolutely perfect all of the time, and better than Sadie, too. He was looking forward to the trials. He was looking forward to how proud Mister would be when Angus had earned a leg. He didn't know what he was going to have to do to get it, but he did remember that a leg was the prize you won. When he thought about it, he understood that he didn't really know what a leg was—except, since Lucy hadn't had any more legs than he did, he figured it couldn't be a real leg. Maybe it was a cast? No, Lucy didn't have a cast. He didn't know what a leg was, but he wanted it. He hoped it wasn't a cast.

Earning a leg was much harder than bringing a sheep home in a snowstorm, Angus was sure. He could barely wait for the day of the trials to come, and when it did, he jumped up into the cab of the truck so eagerly that Missus said, "I guess he really does want to compete."

"Of course," Mister said. "He's been working hard. He's ready to show off."

After Mister and Angus drove away, Missus and Sadie went back inside to finish cleaning up after breakfast, to put the laundry into the dryer, and to make the bed, before starting on the garden. Starting on the garden meant putting pairs of stakes into the ground and tying string between them. The seeds would be planted in straight lines right under those strings. Starting on the garden meant cutting up the seedling potatoes and planting them in the ground, and then mounding the dirt up over them into tiny hills. It was also supposed to mean getting the tomato seedlings planted, but by then it had started to rain, so Missus and Sadie went back inside the house.

Missus washed up and had lunch. She folded laundry and then she sat to sew her quilt, while Sadie had a nap. Later, they raced together through the rain down to the barn to milk the cows and give them fresh water. Then they raced together back to the house, Missus splashing up the path and Sadie splashing right beside her. On the porch, Missus took off her boots and then dried off all four of Sadie's paws on a towel before either one of them went into the warm kitchen.

That night, Sadie stayed in the house with Missus. While Missus had a long hot bath, Sadie had a nap in the steamy warm bathroom, right beside the tub. Sadie slept upstairs that night on the rug beside Missus's bed. She and Missus listened to the rain while Missus read her book. At last Missus said, "I hope it's not raining like this in Massachusetts. The news says it isn't, and I hope it's right for once. Good night, Sadie."

Sadie wagged her tail, a soft thump-thump on the floor.

It was raining when they woke up, so after the cows were
taken care of and the ironing was done, and the bed was
made and the house vacuumed, they still couldn't plant
tomatoes. Instead, "Come on, Sadie," Missus said, and
she went upstairs again. "I don't know. I just don't know,
so I need your help."

Sadie followed, ready to help.

The job was: to sit quietly for a long time in every
spare room. There were three spare rooms that needed
sitting in. "Let's get the feel of this room," Missus said at
the door of the first as they went in.

Sadie didn't know what getting the feel was, but she
was happy to go along. It turned out that getting the feel
of a room meant sitting on the bed for a while, and then
lying down on it to look up at the ceiling. It meant sitting in the chair and looking at the floor and the walls,
and then getting up to look in the closet. Getting the feel
meant looking out the windows for a while, opening
them to smell the air, and closing them before too much
rain could get in.

"If you were a baby, would you want a room that
faced east for the sunrise?" Missus asked. "Or west for
the sunset?"

Sadie didn't know, but she remembered, *The baby at
Thanksgiving just wanted to sleep.*

"If you were a baby, would you want a big room with lots of space in it? Or a small, cozy one?" Missus asked, and Sadie didn't know that either. *How long will the baby be staying?*

Missus didn't know at first, but she knew by the end of the morning for sure. She asked Sadie next about what color walls the baby would want, or if a baby preferred wallpaper.

Color? Wallpaper?

"Thanks, Sadie," Missus said. "You've been a big, big help. And look, the rain is stopping."

After lunch they could go back to the garden to plant the seedling tomatoes and peppers.

"Tomorrow we'll plant peas and carrots," Missus said. "I wonder how Angus is getting on. Do you think he'll do all right?"

Of course! He'll be perfect!

"They'll be home tonight," Missus said, "so we'll find out then."

It was late, long after supper, when Angus and Mister returned. Missus and Sadie were waiting for them in the kitchen. Mister and Missus were so glad to see each other that they both talked at the same time. "Is everything okay? How are you three?" "How did Angus like it? What about you, how did you like the trials?"

Sadie forgot that Angus didn't want to talk to her. *You're back! I'm glad you're back!*

And Angus had forgotten that he was angry. *I was good! I was perfect at standing for exam! The judge said I was a rare one. But sometimes I couldn't remember,* he told her. *Sometimes I got distracted. Like you.* ..

But you never get distracted.

When I heeled on the leash, I was perfect! And a lot of people watched, and they applauded. Sometimes they made me do it wrong and that felt bad. It's all right when you do it wrong, but not me.

Mister was telling Missus, "I hadn't trained him to finish properly, so of course he couldn't do it. It was my fault. But you should have heard the judge, he was really impressed with Angus. A whole lot of the dogs were disqualified from the long sit and down because they got into a fight. But Angus held it perfectly, no matter what the others did. He was the only one to get an excellent score on that one, weren't you, boy?"

I was the only one! And it was hard! They all growled and snarled and bit. You would have been frightened, Sadie, at all the barking, all the noise, and all those strangers.

Sadie disagreed. *Maybe not.*

When Sadie argued with him about something she didn't know anything about, Angus tasted angry again, in his mouth. But he wanted to talk about the trial, to remember it again, and Sadie was the only one who could listen to him. He wanted to tell Sadie about it more than he wanted to be angry with her so he let the anger go away. *Maybe not. But probably. But I had to do everything, like when we do training here, only there was a whole row of us doing it at the same time. You know what was the hardest?*

The long down? Sadie guessed. That would have been the hardest for her.

Heel off the leash, Angus told her.

But you're really good at heel, Sadie told him. *You like heel.*

I know. It was still the hardest. He tried to explain. *I didn't know I shouldn't listen when the judge talked.*

But you had Mister there, to help you.

*But Mister wasn't the one who had to do it. It was all up to only me. It was sort of lonely, and—*Angus was trying to figure out what he wanted to say.

I think I know, Sadie said.

When I got it right it was sort of exciting, but—

Like that sheep this winter in the woods, Sadie said.

Frightening. Because it was all up to me, he remembered.

I know.

You know because of that sheep this winter. Angus was

really glad Sadie could understand how hard it had been to be in a trial. He guessed that sometimes it might be all right for her not to obey—but he didn't think he could ever learn that. He didn't think he *wanted* to learn that, either. It was like the way Sadie couldn't learn to fetch, he realized. Then he realized something else. *We're not the same!* he said. *We're different!*

I know.

Missus called Angus over, to pet and praise him. "He says you'll probably get a leg next time. Good for you, Angus." Mister called Sadie over to pet her, too, and to praise her for being good company for Missus. "I hear you were a big help with planting, or at least with the digging. Good dog, Sadie."

All of the attention, added to being home together, made Angus and Sadie more and more excited, until Mister stood up, opened the door, and said, "Outside, both of you. Go burn off some of that energy while I finish telling your mistress about the trial and the herding dog exhibition. You should have seen them, honey," he said.

The dogs ran through the door and down the porch stairs. They ran down the path to the barn and back to the garden and then a little way down the driveway. The night was dark, but not at all cold. They ran up and down the driveway, first Angus chasing Sadie and then

Sadie chasing Angus. Then they ran in circles around the grassy field behind the garden until they were tired enough to stop.

While they rested in the grass, Angus told Sadie, *It's a bad feeling, feeling frightened. It's . . . uncomfortable.*

I remember, Sadie said.

Like you and the cats, Angus said. Actually, now that he was used to it, he thought maybe he liked Sadie being brave enough to chase after the barn cats. He even liked her brave and clever enough to rescue the sheep from the storm. It could actually be more fun for him that way, and for her, too, even though she could probably never be well enough trained to earn a leg in a trial.

Do you know what I saw? he asked.

No, what?

There were dogs that herded sheep. Really, they did, they really herded them, and the sheep went where the dogs wanted them to.

I can do that, Sadie said. *I did that.*

Angus wanted to object, because it wasn't the same as the dogs at the trials. It couldn't have been. But he couldn't object because it really had happened, and he knew that. *Mister should teach me how, and you, too. Because dogs can herd the sheep together. With two of us, we would never lose any, not ever.*

Maybe Sadie already understood something about

sheep that Angus didn't know. He wasn't sure about that, but he knew that if she did, she would want to show him.

Sadie remembered that she had news of her own to tell. *They're having a baby. I know what room the baby will sleep in.* Then she also remembered, *I was a big help!*

I thought you didn't like children.

Sadie explained, *This isn't children. This is a baby.*

Some things Sadie might know about, but others she didn't, so Angus explained it to her. *Babies grow, and when they do they turn into children.*

I don't believe that, Sadie said, but she knew that while Angus didn't know everything, he knew a lot, so she guessed she should believe it. *Maybe, if it started out only a baby, I could still like it when it was a child. Do you think I could?*

It's going to be a lot of responsibility, Angus said. *And work.*

It's going to be a lot of fun, said Sadie.

Angus guessed Sadie was right, but he knew he was righter. *Let's go back to the house. But not a race,* he said. *Because we're not racing against each other, are we?*

Sadie didn't get it. *I'm racing with you, and you're racing with me,* she said. She barked for the excitement of it all and turned to run. *Let's go!*

The two dogs ran back across the field toward the house, with Angus ahead and Sadie catching up.